Praise for Graham Masterton

"One of the few true masters of the horror genre."
—James Herbert

"Masterton is a crowd pleaser, filling his pages
with sparky, appealing dialogue and visceral grue."
—*Time Out* (London)

"Graham Masterton's novels are charming,
dangerous, and frightening . . . but all based on
enormous erudition." —*L'Express* (Paris)

"One of the most original and frightening
storytellers of our time." —Peter James

GRAHAM MASTERTON

TRAUMA

A SIGNET BOOK

SIGNET
Published by New American Library, a division of
Penguin Putnam Inc., 375 Hudson Street,
New York, New York 10014, U.S.A.
Penguin Books Ltd, 80 Strand,
London WC2R 0RL, England
Penguin Books Australia Ltd, Ringwood,
Victoria, Australia
Penguin Books Canada Ltd, 10 Alcorn Avenue,
Toronto, Ontario, Canada M4V 3B2
Penguin Books (N.Z.) Ltd, 182–190 Wairau Road,
Auckland 10, New Zealand

Penguin Books Ltd, Registered Offices:
Harmondsworth, Middlesex, England

First published by Signet, an imprint of New American Library,
a division of Penguin Putnam Inc.

First Printing, January 2002
10 9 8 7 6 5 4 3 2 1

PUBLISHER'S NOTE
This is a work of fiction. Names, characters, places, and incidents either
are the product of the author's imagination or are used fictitiously,
and any resemblance to actual persons, living or dead, business
establishments, events, or locales is entirely coincidental.

"But she was of the world where the fairest things have the worst fate. Like a rose, she lived as long as roses live, the space of one morning."

—Francois de Malherbe

THE DAY'S REQUIREMENTS

Bonnie went into the garage to collect the extra sprays she needed for this morning's job. They were arranged neatly on shelves on the left-hand side, with the bleaches and biological agents right at the top, for safety. She fitted them into a blue plastic milk crate.

Fantastik multisurface cleaner
Resolve carpet stain remover
Woolite upholstery shampoo
Windex window and glass cleaner
Lysol disinfectant
Glade Odor Neutralizer (nonfragranced)

She sang, "Love, ageless and evergreen . . . seldom seen . . . by two."

At the rear of the garage stood her washing machine and tumble dryer, and all of her household cleaning things, her dusters and her scrubbing brushes and her cans of polish. On the right-hand side of the garage, which was Duke's side, just as the right-hand side of the bed was Duke's side, stood a dusty Honda Black Bomber motorcycle with its rear wheel detached. Countless cans of motor oil were crowded against the wall, and the shelves were littered with wrenches and motorcycle repair manuals with greasy thumbprints on them, as well as half-empty bottles of Coors Lite and peanut butter jars filled with rusty nuts and bolts. On the wall hung a *Playboy* Playmate calendar for 1997, with curled-up edges. It had been turned over no farther than Miss February, and a heavy red circle had been drawn around Thursday the fifteenth.

Bonnie would never forget February 15, 1997. That was the day Duke had been given the sack.

THE GLASS HOUSE

At 11:42 she arrived at the Glass house. She was over twenty minutes late because of the traffic on the Santa Monica Freeway. She parked her big old Dodge truck outside and jumped down from the cab.

The insurance adjuster was waiting for her in his car with the engine running to keep the air-conditioning going. He climbed out and put on his sunglasses. He was young and very thin, with a white short-sleeved shirt and arms as pale as chicken legs.

"Ms. Winter? I'm Dwight Frears from Western Domestic Insurance."

"Pleased to know you," said Bonnie. "Sorry I kept you waiting."

"Well—waiting, ma'am." He grinned. "That's an integral part of my job."

The morning was very hot, touching 103. The sky was bronze with smog. Bonnie walked across the scrubby, unkempt grass in front of the Glass house and stood with her hands on her hips, looking it over. Dwight Frears came and stood beside her, persistently clicking his ballpoint pen.

"Sheriff Kellett said this happened just over a week ago," said Bonnie.

"Yes, ma'am." Dwight Frears checked his clipboard. "July eighth to be precise."

Bonnie shaded her eyes with her hand. The Glass house was identical to hundreds of others in this part of San Bernardino. A shingle roof, a Spanish-style porch, a garage with a bent basketball hoop. The only difference was that this house was badly neglected— its air-conditioner rusted, its screen doors perforated, its light green stucco beginning to peel.

Bonnie approached the front windows and tried to peer through the slats of the grimy green venetian blinds. All she could see was a sagging white vinyl couch and her own reflection: a full-figured woman of thirty-four with bright strawberry-blond hair wearing a black Elvis T-shirt and a pair of white jeans with a stretch waistband.

Dwight consulted his clipboard again. "What the coroner's office said was . . . the kids were found in the back bedroom. One on the bed and one on the hideaway."

Bonnie walked around the side of the house, lifting a makeshift wash line with one hand. At the back there was a small yard with a play set, two sun loungers and a grease-encrusted barbecue. A child's tricycle was tipped over on its side.

She could see into the kitchen. Apart from the number of flies that were crawling all over it, it looked like any other kitchen. The back bedroom window, however, was covered by what looked like a shimmering black curtain. Dwight was about to say something, but then he realized what it was and turned to Bonnie with that look on his face.

Bonnie walked back around to the front of the house. "Okay . . . it looks like mostly the back bedroom and a general cleanup of everyplace else. We're talking six hours minimum, which comes out at twelve hundred plus materials plus transportation, say a round fifteen hundred."

Dwight sounded as if he were having trouble breathing. "Fifteen hundred? Sounds about right to me."

They sat in his car to fill out the insurance forms. He had almost finished when another car drew up, a battered blue Datsun with one brown door. A small, birdlike woman with a large nose and flicked-up hair climbed out and rapped on the passenger window.

"Hi, Bonnie. Sorry I'm late."

"Hi, Ruth. This is Dwight."

"Hi, Dwight."

Dwight signed the estimate and handed it over without a word.

Once Dwight had left, Bonnie and Ruth went to the back of the truck. It was loaded with gallon containers of industrial disinfectant, rolls of green plastic sheeting, stacks of heavy-duty garbage bags, insecticide sprays and plastic carryalls stocked with bleaches and spray solvents.

"You and Duke sort things out?" asked Ruth as she took out a bright yellow plastic suit and began to step into it.

"I guess. But I don't know. Duke's so *weird* these days. It's like he's been taken over by the body snatchers. If I didn't think he was too darn lazy, I'd say that he was seeing another woman."

Bonnie tugged on her protective suit, too. It was clammy at the best of times, but in this heat she was sweating all over before she had even zipped it up. She sat on the truck's front bumper to pull on her rubber boots.

"You know what happened here?" Ruth asked her.

"Not exactly. Jack Kellett said there was a fight over custody. The wife was determined not to let her husband have the kids. The next thing they knew, the neighbors reported a smell coming from the house, and they found the wife gone and both kids dead."

Ruth handed Bonnie a respirator and put one on herself. They walked toward the house carrying their two-gallon insecticide spray can and their garbage bags. The street had been almost deserted until now, but a man came out opposite to start washing his car, and another couple came out and started paying exaggerated attention to their lawn sprinkler. Three teenagers started to skateboard around the Glass house, circling closer and closer.

Bonnie's thighs rubbed together with a plasticky squeaking noise, and her breathing inside the respirator sounded as if an asthmatic were following her across the grass. She reached the front door and took out the key that had been given to her by the realty company. There was a brass knocker on the front door in the shape of a large beetle. She opened up and they went inside.

It was an ordinary, shabby little house. There was a narrow entrance corridor, with a door on the left leading off to the front room and a door on the right leading to a bedroom. Ahead of them the kitchen door was slightly ajar.

The house was teeming with flies. They were crawling over everything—the walls, the furniture, the windows. Bonnie nudged Ruth and mimed the action of vacuum cleaning. Ruth gave her a thumbs-up and went in search of the broom closet.

Hanging in the hall was a large wooden crucifix with a plaster Christ nailed onto it and a wooden plaque with *God Bless The Children* etched into it. Bonnie went into the living room, with its white vinyl furniture and a television the size of the Los Angeles County courthouse. The smell was much more noticeable in here, even though Bonnie's respirator spared her from the worst of it. Before she started this job, she had never realized how strongly human beings smelled when they died. Even dried blood, on its own, had a stench like rotten chicken.

Sometimes in the middle of the night she lay awake and wondered how people could love each other, considering how perishable they were, and what they were really like inside.

She crossed the living room rug. It was a matted beige shag, with a crisscross pattern of brown footprints on it, like dance-lesson instructions. She went through to the kitchen, batting flies away from her face. A head of iceberg lettuce on the draining board had turned into a lump of yellow slime. A knife lay beside it, ready to cut it up for salad.

Inside the back bedroom she came across the children's toys, scattered on the floor. A Fisher-Price pull-along telephone. A bright blue dump truck, carrying bricks. There was a single bed against the wall and a hide-a-bed at right angles to it. So many flies were clustered on the window that she had to switch on the overhead light. There were two shiny brown stains, like wood varnish, one on each bed.

Bonnie picked up one of the extra-heavy-duty plastic sacks. She reached up and dragged down the drapes and folded them roughly into it, along with scores of glittering emerald flies. At that moment, Ruth came in with the vacuum cleaner. She plugged it in and started to suck away the flies around the hide-a-bed as matter-of-factly as if she were cleaning up her own house.

They tore down all the drapes and all the blinds. "Save these?" asked Ruth, with an armful of faded gold velour.

"Sure. I'll take those down to the trash."

They carried the beds out to Bonnie's truck and laid them one on top of the other like a sandwich so that the neighbors couldn't see the stains. They ripped up all the carpets and rolled them up ready for toting away.

The carpet in the children's room was the worst. When Bonnie pulled it away from the wall, its underlay was seething with maggots, and Ruth had to sweep them up with a dustpan and brush.

Everything went into the plastic garbage sacks. Books, bank statements, family photographs, newspapers, clothing, birthday cards. A crayon drawing of two small boys under a spiky yellow sun and the words *We Love You, Mom*. Bonnie was glad that there were no grieving relatives here today, the way there sometimes were. It was bad enough cleaning up after somebody's death without having to explain why God had allowed it to happen.

Ruth came in from the bathroom. She was holding up a hypodermic syringe.

Bonnie took off her respirator. She opened her sack a little wider and said, "Just drop it in here. I'll tell Dan about it later."

Ruth took off her respirator, too. "It was in the laundry. You never know, it might be important."

Bonnie didn't say anything. Occasionally she came across evidence that the police had overlooked, but she didn't make a religion of reporting it. She was a cleaner, not a cop, and in this business there wasn't much future in letting too many people know that she might have figured out more than was good for her. She had been threatened twice by her own clients: once when she had found some burned fragments of letters in the fireplace; the second time when she had taken a phone call in a house in Topanga Canyon, asking, urgently, "Is she dead yet?"

After two-and-a-half hours, the Glass house was clean enough for them to stand outside for a while and drink strong black coffee, which Ruth had brought with her in a flask. The neighbors continued to watch them, and now they had even stopped pretending that they were trimming their hedges, but none of them came near.

"Where're you going to dump all this?" asked Ruth, nodding toward the beds and the carpets piled up on the back of the truck.

"It's not biohazard. I'll take it to Riverside."

"I thought Riverside was squeamish about maggots."

"*I'm* squeamish about maggots. But I'll give Mr. Hatzopolous my sweetest smile."

She tipped the dregs of her coffee into the gutter and went back inside. There was only the master bedroom to finish off now. It was a cheap imitation of a Niagara Falls honeymoon suite, with cream chipboard furniture with imitation-gilt handles and a pink padded headboard on the bed with two yellowish stains on it from heads that had once rested while the bed's occupants sat up and watched TV.

In one corner stood a spindly dressing table with a crowd of half-used cosmetics on it, as well as a china ballerina with her upraised foot missing. Right in the center of the dressing table was one of those Mexican sugar skulls from the Day of the Dead, with a bite taken out of it.

Bonnie took hold of the grubby white throw and dragged it back. She crammed it into a garbage sack and then reached for the pillows. As she picked the first one up, she found something black clinging to the edge of it, and then another, and another. She shook the pillow in disgust, and six or seven more fell out. They were shiny and brittle, with a pointed, twisted shape like seashells—dark brown rather than black, and faintly translucent, so that she could see that there was something inside them. It was only when she picked one up and looked at it more closely that she realized what it was: a chrysalis. A butterfly, or a moth maybe, or some other insect.

It must have been the hot weather, she guessed. Last week, cleaning up an apartment on Franklin Avenue, she had come across a mass of huge blowfly larvae, much bigger than any she had ever encountered before. Ruth had said it was an omen, although she didn't know what of. Ruth was deeply superstitious for somebody who spent her time scrubbing the blood of suicides out of people's upholstery.

THE NECESSARY INGREDIENTS

Bonnie took out the recipe book that her mother had given her when she and Duke were first married. *Home Cooking For Brides,* by Hannah Mathias. The cover was torn, and it fell open at Meat Loaf, which was Duke's favorite. However, she turned to the next chapter, which was Poultry, and found the recipe she had been reading over the weekend.

One chicken, cut into eight pieces
Two cloves garlic
1 green bell pepper
¼ teaspoon ground cloves
2 teaspoons chili powder
1½ cups chopped canned tomatoes
⅓ cup raisins

4 tablespoons dry sherry
⅓ cup green olives, chopped

She put on her reading glasses while she was following the recipe, and she bent over the book with a concentrated frown.

THE WINTER HOUSE

"So what do you call this?" Duke wanted to know, scrutinizing a piece of chicken on the end of his fork.

"Mexican chicken," said Bonnie, without looking up.

Duke dropped his fork back onto his plate. He sat there with his eyes riveted on Bonnie for almost ten seconds before he demanded, "Tell me something, Bonnie. Do I look to you like a Mexican person? I mean, in any respect?"

Bonnie didn't answer, but went on eating with her eyes fixed on her plate. Between them, their son, Ray, instinctively sat back, as if he were edging himself out of the line of fire.

"Excuse me," Duke persisted. "Have you noticed me wearing a sombrero lately?"

"No, Duke. I haven't noticed you wearing a sombrero lately."

"I mean, I don't have a droopy mustache, do I, or a poncho, and I don't go around saying '*Arriba! Arriba!*' do I?"

"No, Duke, you don't."

"So I don't look like a Mexican person?"

"No." Her throat was so constricted that she could hardly swallow. She knew exactly what he was going to say next and she knew what it was going to lead to, but she didn't know how to stop it.

"I see. You don't think that I look like a Mexican person. So why are you giving me this Mexican food?"

Bonnie lifted her head. "You eat Italian. I don't see your gondola tied up outside."

He stared at her in exaggerated disbelief. "Is this you trying to be funny? My great-grandfather was Italian. Eating Italian, that's in my blood."

"You eat Szechuan, too. Don't tell me you're part Chinese."

"Why do you always have to be so cute? Why can't you answer a simple question with a straightforward answer? I mean, *ever*? Gondola—what's the matter with you? All I said was, what was this stuff you just served up and you said Mexican and I said I'm not a Mexican person and I don't even *look* like a Mexican person, which makes me wonder why you served it up just to annoy me or what?"

Ray muttered, "*I* like it."

Duke opened his arms to heaven. "Oh, that's wonderful. *You* like it. Shows how much of a gourmet you're not. And why do you always side with your mother? That's a personal insult you're eating. That's a personal insult to me. Why don't you just admit it? You'd rather eat something that made you sick to your stomach than agree with your old man, wouldn't you? Well, I hope it sticks in your throat, the both of you!"

He threw down his napkin, scraped back his chair and pushed his way out of the kitchen. The swing door *twang*-thumped backward and forward and then stopped. Bonnie sat looking at her meal, her fork poised, not moving. The overhead light made her look as if she were in a play. Ray continued to eat for a while; then he gave up, too.

"Did you really like it?" asked Bonnie.

"Hey, it was great." She noticed that he had picked out all the raisins and left them around the rim of his plate.

They cleaned up, scraping the remaining food into the sink. There was still quite a lot left in the pot, but Bonnie emptied that into the sink, too. She washed the plates in silence for a while. Ray stood beside her with a dish towel, waiting to dry them, tall, blinking, with coat-hanger shoulders and hair that always looked as if he had just woken up.

He was seventeen years old, the same age that she had been when she had given birth to him. She found it almost impossible to believe. Had she really been that young?

Tonight Ray was wearing his favorite T-shirt with LA CORONERS DEPT printed on it. Duke hated it, or said that he hated it. "I hate that. You want people to think you've got unhealthy interests, or what?"

Bonnie stacked the plates into the hutch. "Your

father's so touchy these days. I'm beginning to think that it's me."

"Why should it be you? What have you done?"

"Tell me what I haven't done. I've started the cleanup business, right? And I'm still holding down my regular job at Glamorex. You can't blame your father for feeling a little inadequate, can you?"

"He could find a job if he wanted to. He doesn't even try. Just sits on his duff all day watching *Days of Our Lives*."

"Come on, Ray. He hasn't worked in over a year now. It's not so much that he's lazy. . . . He's just kind of out of the loop."

"That still doesn't give him the right to take it out on you."

"I'm a big girl now, Ray. I can take stuff like that."

Unexpectedly, Ray came up to her and put his arms around her and pressed his cheek against her shoulder.

"What?" she said.

"Nothing. I just wish that you and Dad could make up."

She found herself stroking his spiky hair. "We will. I promise you. We're going through a difficult time, that's all. Everybody goes through difficult times."

"But it's every day. It's every single day."

Bonnie snapped off her bright yellow rubber gloves. "Never mind. How about a cup of coffee?"

Ray lifted his head and looked up at her. "Do you mind if I ask you a personal question?"

She laid both hands on his shoulders, smiling. "You can ask me anything you like. I'm your mother."

"Dad—you know—do you still, like, *love* him?"

Bonnie looked into Ray's eyes and they were the same color as hers: palest faded blue—the blue of cornflowers found pressed between the pages of a family Bible.

"That's a very complex thing to ask me," she said. "And all I can say is . . . there are lots of different answers, and even *I* don't know what they are."

"I knew you'd chicken out."

"Oh, yes? At least I didn't Mexican chicken out."

He came bursting into the bedroom at 2:34 in the morning, stinking of beer and cigarette smoke. She lay in bed pretending to sleep while he tilted and ricocheted from one side of the room to the other. His shoes tumbled across the floor and then—shackled by the legs of his pants—he fell full length onto the bed, right beside her.

"Bonnie . . ." he breathed. His breath was so rancid that she had to turn her face away. "Bonnie, listen to me. I love you. You don't even know how much I love you. You don't have any—*shit*!" he said, as he tried to kick his pants off his ankles.

"*Know* we always argue—*know* that, baby. But it's not always me. Sometimes—sometimes it's you. I mean you work all day and you work all night and you hardly even look at me and think, That's my man. That's my *man*. And a man . . . *needs* that kind of reassurance, baby. Needs that kind of respect. And what happens to me? I'll tell you what happens to me. I lose my job to some wetback. And then my wife—my dear devoted wife of seventeen years, my

baby, my queen—what does she do? She rubs . . .
she rubs salt in the wound, man. That's what she
does. *Salt*. Not only does she cut off my nuts, she
serves them up for dinner and calls them *cojones*."

He clenched his fist and began to pound the pillow. Spit was flying from his mouth, and Bonnie
pulled up the sheet to protect her face. She wasn't
frightened. She just wanted him to stop shouting and
let her get some sleep.

"Mexican chicken, for Christ's sake! Mexican
chicken! I mean, like, twist the knife or what? Don't
you think I feel—*nothing* enough already?"

Bonnie turned over and put her arm around him.
"Duke, you're drunk. Try to get some sleep."

"You think I'm drunk? I'm not even half drunk.
I'm—I'm—*injured*."

Bonnie stroked the back of his neck. "Injured," he
told the pillow, with even greater vehemence. "I'm
injured."

In the dark, Bonnie could still picture what he
looked like when they first dated. Thin, almost effem-
inate, with a high black pompadour and such a cool
way of walking and talking. He was funny, he was
sharp, he was always the center of attention. He
could blow twenty smoke rings, one after another.
His friends always called him The Dook and mock-
bowed whenever they met him. But even The Dook
grew older and left school and had to find work; and
that was when The Dook discovered that being able
to blow smoke rings was no substitute for having
vocational qualifications. The best job that he could
find was rewiring automobiles—and then, when he

asked for a fifty-cent raise, the company sacked him and brought in a Mexican electrician instead, for two dollars an hour less.

He raised his head. In the dim light from the bedside alarm clock, his face was glistening with tears. "You're not going to leave me, are you, Bonnie? You still love me, don't you?"

"Will you hush up and get some sleep? I have to be up by six."

"You don't have anybody else, do you, Bonnie? I've seen the way that Ralph Kosherick looks at you. Like his eyes are bulging out and his goddamned tongue's dragging on the rug. You wouldn't screw Ralph Kosherick, would you, Bonnie? Tell me you wouldn't screw Ralph Kosherick!"

"For Christ's sake, Duke, will you stop?"

She closed her eyes and tried to think about something else. Every time Duke got drunk, he raged about Ralph, and the truth was that Ralph was smart and presentable and even attractive in a rather too brotherly kind of way, but there must have been something that Duke saw in Ralph that represented everything he hated to the point of incandescence. Education, and middle-class values, and pants that only just skimmed the tops of his shoes.

"I'm telling you, Bonnie. I could take Ralph Kosherick by the neck and I could physically strangle him, I promise you."

"Duke, you're drunk."

He sat up like a Polaris missile going off. *"Drunk?"* he roared. *"Drunk?"* He grabbed the pillows and threw them across the room. "I'm your husband and I'm trying to tell you how much I hurt inside, and I'm *drunk?* Well, *excuse* me! Maybe I should just forget about trying to talk to you and do what Ralph Kosherick does to you!"

"Duke, sweetheart, will you please just stop shouting? I have to get up early tomorrow and Ray has school."

"Who *gives* a shit?" Duke screamed at her. "I don't have to get up for anything! I could lie in bed all day and it wouldn't make any difference!"

"Duke—"

Without warning, he dragged back the sheet, climbed on top of her, and pulled up her nightgown. The clock faintly illuminated her big, rounded breasts and her big, rounded stomach. She said, "Duke— no—" and tried to pull her nightgown down again, but Duke forced her thighs apart.

"You and that goddamned Ralph Kosherick. You and that—*goddamned*—Ralph—Kosherick."

She felt him between her legs, as soft as a baby mouse. He put his hand down and tried to squish himself into her, but he couldn't. He pushed his hips forward, grunting with effort. Bonnie lay patiently and waited for him to stop trying, which he eventually did. He dropped on top of her and sobbed into her ear, his stubble scratching her neck and his tears dripping over her shoulder.

She gave him little pecking kisses and stroked his pompadour. It was so much thinner these days.

Things to Do on
Wednesday

Bonnie kept a small Ninja Turtles notebook in her purse, which Ray had given her when he was twelve. There were only a few pages left, and she was going to hint that she needed a new one soon. She took out her red ballpoint pen and made a list of everything she had to do today.

Collect dry cleaning from Star-Tex
Remind Ralph about Moist-Your-Eyes promotion
Meet Susan for lunch 1:30
Collect truck tire
Buy pork chops, ice cream, bathroom tissue
Call Mike Paretti re insecticide

She had heard from Pfizer that there was a powerful new chemical for clearing out screwworms and she was interested to know if Mike had tried it. She was disgusted by maggots and blowflies and other parasitical insects, but at the same time she found them fascinating. An expert entomological pathologist could often tell from the parasites in a person's body just when they had died, and how, and even where they had been killed. There was something else about parasites, too. It was their total disregard for human beauty and human tragedy. They were blind to everything but their own appetites.

THE DAY JOB

Ray came into the kitchen, yawning, his hair sticking up like Stan Laurel's. He opened the fridge and stared into it for almost half a minute. Then he closed it again.

Bonnie finished off her list, folded it and tucked it into her purse. "You're up early."

"Urgghhh . . . I have to finish my math homework."

"Your father didn't keep you awake, did he?"

"Only me and half of greater Los Angeles."

He took a loaf of bread out of the larder and spread three slices with peanut butter, almost a half inch thick. Then he cut up two bananas and arranged them on top of each slice. He switched on the television, folded up the first slice of bread and started to eat it. He ate the same thing every morning. He had

read in some men's health magazine that bananas
and peanut butter helped you to put on weight.

The kitchen was painted bright yellow, with bright
yellow checkered curtains. In the morning sunshine,
it looked like the set for a 1960s cornflakes commercial. Sydney Omarr, the psychic, had once told Bonnie that yellow was her lucky color. He had also told
her that she would see more death than most people
see in thirteen lifetimes. She hadn't believed him, but
that was four years, before she had started Bonnie's
Trauma Scene Clean.

She said, "Your father'll get over this. You wait
and see."

"Oh, yeah?" Ray was absorbed in watching *Scooby
Doo*.

"He's a good man, really. He finds life . . . *confus-
ing*, that's all."

She stood by the sink, finishing her decaf. She
looked at Ray, expecting him to turn around and say
something, but he didn't. After a while she tipped
away the rest of her coffee, rinsed her mug and gave
him a kiss on top of his chaotic, sweaty hair. "I'll
see you at six. I shouldn't be later than that. Pork
chops tonight."

" 'Kay, Mom."

There was a pause. Then she said, "Ray."

He didn't answer. He knew what she was going
to say, and she knew he knew.

She said it all the same. "I love you, Ray. Things
are going to get better."

Outside the house, the driveway was only just
wide enough to accommodate their two vehicles:

Bonnie's Dodge truck and Duke's eleven-year-old Buick Electra. When they had first moved in, Bonnie had imagined that they would live here for two or three years and then buy someplace much more spacious, with a pool that you could swim more than two-and-a-half strokes in before you hit the concrete edge on the other side, and the neighbors' barbecue smoke didn't billow in through your kitchen window. She had imagined four or five orange trees, a hot tub, and maybe even a view.

That was thirteen years ago, when Ray was only four years old. She didn't think about the four or five orange trees or the hot tub anymore, and she didn't expect a better view than a gray-painted fence. But she kept on selling Glamorex cosmetics and she kept on scrubbing away the stains of other people's traumas, and she knew that she had to be working so doggedly for *some* reason, although she would never allow herself to face up to what it was.

She liked Barbra Streisand. She liked "Evergreen" so much that she played it over and over. Not when Duke was around, though.

She drove over to Venice Boulevard in Duke's Electra. The air-conditioning didn't work, and the seats were patched with silver duct tape. By the time she reached Venice Boulevard, her blouse was sticking to her back. She found a parking space only half a block away from the Glamorex offices. As she hurried along the sidewalk, an elderly man in a white golfing cap gave her a wide, denture-crowded smile. A real geriatric, about eighty-five years old. "Say there. Nice gazongas."

At first her brain didn't register what he had said.

But then she stopped and turned around and called out, "Hey!" The sidewalk was empty. She almost thought that she must have imagined it. She hesitated for a moment, frowning, but then she pushed her way through the revolving doors into the ice-cold lobby and click-clacked her way across the polished marble floor to the elevators.

Up on the fourteenth floor, headquarters of Glamorex of Hollywood, Inc., dozens of cardboard boxes were stacked all over the reception area and along the corridor. Joyce Bach, the distribution manager, was standing in the middle of all this chaos with her frizzy black hair looking even more disorganized than ever. A half-smoked cigarette dangled from her glossy red lips (Scarlet Siesta), and every time she spoke she dropped ash on her royal-blue suit.

"Would you believe it? They've delivered less than half of the fall hair-color range. And they've printed the Millennium Face-Glow packaging upside-down. Like, who's running this operation, orangutans?"

Ralph Kosherick came out, holding a clipboard and looking harassed. He was a tall man with slightly stooping shoulders and a big, rumpled Fred Mac-Murray kind of face. Every time she talked to him, Bonnie felt an overwhelming urge to take out her nail scissors and trim his shaggy black eyebrows. He wore a white shirt with the sleeves rolled up and purple suspenders that kept his the cuffs of his pants flapping an inch above his polished black Oxfords.

"You're late, Bonnie," he said, without checking his watch. "But . . . since you look so ravishing this morning, I'll forgive you."

"I hope you say things like that to your wife."

"Of course I say things like that to my wife. I just make sure that she's out of earshot. Don't want her getting big-headed."

"You're a terrible man, Ralph. Where am I scheduled today?"

He flapped his way through the papers on his clipboard. "I want you to make a call to Marshall's first, and then go over to Hoffman Drugs to see what new stock they need. I've moved your Millennium promotion to three o'clock."

"Okay, that suits me better. I have a lunch date at one-thirty."

"Cancel it. Let me take you. I've found this new place on Melrose where they do stuffed vine leaves to die for. Meet me back here when you've finished at Hoffman."

"Ralph, that's very generous of you. But like I've said before, I think we ought to keep our relationship on a strict professional basis."

"I like the sound of strict. I'm not too sure about professional."

"Won't your wife ever beat you?"

"Vanessa? Are you kidding? She can't even beat me at Scrabble."

Bonnie collected her boxes of samples, and LeRoy, the mail boy, helped her carry them down to the street. He had a personal stereo in his ears and he moonwalked toward her car in time to his faintly heard music. Bonnie had to slam the trunk of Duke's car three times to shut it, and then she said, "What's that you're listening to?"

LeRoy lifted one earphone and frowned at her as if he didn't know who she was. "Say what?"

"I said, what's that you're listening to?"

He handed the earphones over and Bonnie listened for a while. Techno dance-beat drumming, endless repetitive riffs, and somebody singing over and over again, "Wake up the dayyudd . . . you kill me bruvva . . . wake up the dayyudd . . ."

She gave the earphones back. "That's very nice. I think I'll stick to Billy Ray Cyrus."

The buyer at Marshall's was a small woman called Doris Feinman, who wore a black suit and so much foundation that she looked like an understudy for a Noh play. She scattered Bonnie's lipstick samples over her desk and took all the caps off and muddled them up.

"What's this one called? Blood Orange? It's an interesting shade, but don't you think it sounds a little *menstrual*?"

"We can change the names. Absolutely no problem."

"Well, that's good news. I don't care for Cranberry Climax either. Who thinks these up?"

Bonnie didn't answer, but kept her mouth fixed in a tight approximation of a smile. Just because Glamorex was one of her smaller suppliers, Doris Feinman always had to go through the same ritual of messing up Bonnie's samples and making scathing comments.

"This eyelash thickener . . . it comes out way too blobby. Women these days don't want to look like Goldie Hawn. It's too mindless, too submissive, don't you think?"

Bonnie was having a difficult time even pretending

to smile. Jesus, she thought. Submissive eyelash thickener?

It took Doris Feinman an hour and a half to choose what she wanted and to place an order. Ralph would be reasonably pleased, over $13,500's worth. But she hadn't taken any of the Millennium Face-Glow. She had tried it on one of her assistants and said it made her look as if she were dead.

THE GOODMAN APARTMENT

She was driving over to Hoffman Drugs when her pager bleeped. It read MEET MUNOZ 8210 DE LONGPRE SOONEST. "Dammit," she said. She took a left on Spaulding Avenue, and then a right, and five blocks farther along De Longpre she saw two police squad cars and a silver Oldsmobile with a red gumball on the roof. A straggle of neighbors and passersby were hanging around outside—the hyenas, Bonnie called them—sniffing out tattered scraps of excitement from somebody else's tragedy.

She climbed out of the car, and one of the officers lifted the police tape so that she could duck underneath. "The cleanup lady, right? Rather you than me, sweet buns." Bonnie gave him the finger.

A sharply sloping concrete forecourt led down to the basement garage. The building itself was a three-story block of apartments, stucco-fronted and painted a rusty ocher. A flight of red tiled steps led up to the front entrance, where Lieutenant Dan Munoz was leaning against the railing, smoking a bright green cigar and talking to Bill Clift from the coroner's department.

Dan saluted Bonnie as she climbed the steps. "Hi, Bonnie. You got here quick." For a police detective, Dan was almost laughably handsome, with curly chestnut hair and a clean-cut, movie-star jawline. It was his eyes, though, that Bonnie tried to avoid. They were brown and liquid, and she always felt that he knew everything about her just by looking at her—from the recipe she was planning to cook that night right down to the washing instructions on the label of her panties.

Today Dan wore a blue silk suit and a splashy red-and-yellow necktie, and he smelled of Giorgio aftershave. He could have been going out to a swanky dinner instead of examining a crime scene. Bill Clift, on the other hand, was freckled and scruffy with a sagging gray linen coat and eyeglasses that had been glued and reglued and finally taped around the bridge with a grubby Band-Aid.

Dan put his arm around Bonnie's shoulders and gave her an affectionate squeeze. "If you get on the scene any faster than this, you'll be able to roll up the rugs before they start murdering each other."

Bonnie nodded toward the half-open front door. "What's the deal?"

"Come inside and I'll show you."

"I don't know. I'm real tied up at the moment. I

only stopped by because I was on my way to Hoffman's."

"Well, it's a shocker, believe me. Three kids—four, seven and nine. The scenario is, the mother's away, seeing her elderly folks in San Clemente. The nanny's been given the night off. The father goes to the kids' bedroom and shoots them at point-blank range with a pump-action shotgun. Then he goes back to the living room, puts the gun in his mouth and redecorates the wall with the back of his head."

"Jesus," said Bonnie. "Any idea why he did it?"

"Just flipped, I guess. Didn't leave a note or nothing."

"Where's the mother now?"

"Still here." He flipped open his notebook. "Mrs. Bernice Goodman, age thirty-six. That's why I called you. She'll be staying with friends this afternoon, but she's pretty anxious to get the place cleaned up as soon as she can."

Bonnie hesitated for a moment. Then she said, "Okay—let me look it over. Are you and your people all done here now?"

"Sure, we're done. Bill, you're done, aren't you?"

"All bagged up and ready to roll."

Dan ushered Bonnie through the front door into a small L-shaped hallway. The walls were cluttered with group photographs of bowling teams, their eyes red, like werewolves, from the camera flash. In one corner stood a large, prickly pot plant and next to it a table crowded with decorative brass paperweights.

"In here," said Dan. "This is the living area. Well, dying area, I should say."

Bonnie found herself in a large, cream-painted room. The vertical slatted blinds had been closed, so the light was muted. The room was furnished in a modern, minimalist style, cream leather upholstery and glass coffee tables. The only exception was an antique-type display cabinet in one corner, fussily filled with rosettes and silver cups and bowling trophies.

Although it was so plain, the room had an atmosphere that made Bonnie draw in her breath, as if she had suddenly stepped up to her chest in cold water. Most of the trauma scenes she attended were weeks or even months old. But here the feeling of violent death was so recent and so overwhelming that for a split second she thought that she would have to turn around and leave and never come back.

"Come on," Dan coaxed her, as if he knew exactly what she was thinking.

On the opposite wall hung a large abstract painting: a blue triangle and a white square and a small red dot. It was titled *Serenity III*. On the facing wall there was a wide, fan-shaped spray of blood and pinkish clots of brain tissue, and a roughly oval hole in the plaster that Bonnie could have fitted her fist into, surrounded by dozens of tiny black speckles. Pellet holes.

The cream leather couch was spattered and smeared all over with blood. As Bonnie walked around it, she could see that the white rug immediately behind it was stained with a glutinous ruby pool. The children's father had shot himself, and what was left of his head had fallen backward so that, juglike, it had emptied his blood all over the floor.

Dan came and stood beside her. "Sure made his mark, didn't he?"

Bonnie nodded. "He surely did. But that's the difference between men and women, isn't it? When women kill themselves, they always make sure they do it on a wipe-clean surface, or in the bathtub. Men—what do they care? They sit right down in the middle of the living room and bang."

"You sound like you take it personal."

"Do I? Maybe I do. It's like adding insult to injury, don't you think? It's like the man saying, 'Not only does my life not matter anymore, and not only does our relationship not matter anymore, but the home we built together, that doesn't matter anymore, either. Who cares if I spray my head all over it?' "

She looked up at him and said, "Yes, Dan, I do take it personal. I'm a woman. And besides, I have to clean it up."

"You won't get that bloodstain out, will you?"

Bonnie hunkered down and ran her hand through the carpet pile. "This is wool and nylon mix. The trouble with wool is, it leaches up blood, and it won't let go. I have a new enzyme solvent I could try . . . but you're going to be left with a brownish mark here no matter what."

She stood up. "I guess it depends on the widow's insurance. She could always shift the couch back to cover it."

Dan raised one eyebrow.

"What?" she said. "I'm trying to be practical, that's all."

"Oh, sure."

"Dan, not every woman can afford to recarpet her home just because her husband was selfish enough to off himself in the middle of the living room."

"I guess." He looked around and shook his head. "It just makes you wonder what went through his mind, doesn't it?"

Bonnie nodded toward the wall. "That was his mind. Look at it now."

"So what do you think that means, when it comes to the bigger picture?"

"I guess it means that there's a whole lot of difference between who we are and what we're made of."

"And?"

"And nothing. Except that I'm relieved to see that this wall has a washable eggshell finish, so the blood won't have soaked right through to the plaster."

"Well, good deal," said Dan. They looked at each other, and they both knew that their hard-cooked offhandedness was only an act. Nobody who walked into this house and saw what had happened here could fail to be horrified. The muted light, the blood, the terrible emptiness. The endless droning of a single fly.

"How about the bedrooms?" asked Bonnie.

THE BEDROOMS

A corridor led from the left-hand side of the living room to the master bedroom, the bathroom and three smaller bedrooms. The smallest bedroom contained a single bed, a desk and a bookshelf. The walls were decorated with pinups of Brad Pitt and Beck. Out of the window there was a view of the side of the next-door garage, with a lone deflated basketball on the roof.

"Nanny's room," said Dan.

He took her through to the end bedroom. It was here that the four-year-old boy and the seven-year-old girl had slept on bunk beds. There was a brown, metallic smell in here—the smell of recently dried blood. The room was prettily wallpapered in blue stripes and knotted pink flowers. A blue-painted toy chest stood under the window, crammed with Barbies and doll's-house furniture and model automobiles and *Star Wars* figures. On the walls were framed prints of *The House That Jack Built* by Randolph Caldecott.

The bunk beds, however, were almost impossible to look at. Both children had been fast asleep in Disney comforters with pictures of the Lion King on them, and these had been blown into bloody blackened shreds, like monstrous flower blossoms. The Lion King still smiled benevolently at Bonnie out of the carnage, here and there. The mattresses of both beds were completely soaked in crimson. There was blood all the way up the walls, and two umbrella-shaped sprays of blood on the ceiling. It was no consolation at all that the children couldn't have known what hit them.

Bonnie picked up a Raggedy Ann doll, only to find that it had a thin string of unidentifiable human tissue draped across its face. Dan was watching her so all she did was put it down again.

"You know, we have a whole lot in common, you and me," said Dan.

"You think so?"

"Maybe we should meet for a drink one evening, talk."

Bonnie turned. "Why would you want to talk to me, Dan? I'm a thirty-four-year-old mother with only three topics of conversation. Cookery, cosmetics and cleaning up messes like this."

She could see that Dan wanted to say something to her, but he didn't. He turned and led the way into the nine-year-old's bedroom. Pink curtains, tied back with bows. A small dressing table, with play cosmetics set out neatly on top of it, as well as three or four nearly finished lipsticks that she must have been given by her mother. Bonnie picked one up. It was Startling Scarlet, by Glamorex.

The bed was the same bloody riot as the other two, but here it looked as if the father's first shot hadn't been immediately fatal. There were handprints on the wall, and the white sheepskin rug beside the bed was matted with blood, so that it looked like a slaughtered animal.

Dan said, "She had half her pelvis blown away, but she tried to escape. She managed to get as far as the window."

"Yes, I can see."

They looked around the bedroom a few moments longer, and then Dan said, "Think you can do it?"

Bonnie nodded. "Let me go talk to the mother."

DISCUSSING TERMS

Mrs. Goodman sat at the kitchen table. A black woman police officer stood beside her, with one hand on her shoulder. Mrs. Goodman was a thin woman with a prominent nose and blond-highlighted hair that was pinned back in a tight French pleat. She wore a black dress with a diamante poodle brooch. She was holding an undrunk mug of coffee in her lap and staring at nothing at all.

Bonnie gave the police officer a little finger wave, and the officer smiled back. "Hi, Martha," she whispered. "Haven't seen you in a coon's age. How's Tyce?"

Dan leaned over Mrs. Goodman and said, "Mrs. Goodman? This is the cleaning lady I was telling you about."

Bonnie leaned over her, too. "Mrs. Goodman? My

name's Bonnie Winter, from Bonnie's the cleaners. If this is all too soon for you, just let me know. I can always call again some other time. But Lieutenant Munoz here said that you wanted to normalize your apartment as soon as possible."

Mrs. Goodman didn't answer at first, didn't look up. "Is she still in shock?" asked Bonnie. "Shouldn't you take her to the hospital?"

But Mrs. Goodman lifted her head and said, "No, no, I'm all right. I want to stay here. This is where my babies died. I want to stay."

Bonnie drew up one of the kitchen chairs and sat down close to her. The sawtoothed shadow of a yucca was nodding up and down on the venetian blind, and for some reason it put Bonnie in mind of a giant parrot. She gently took away Mrs. Goodman's coffee mug and set it down on the table.

"Why do you think he did it?" Mrs. Goodman asked her, after a while.

"I guess only two people know that, Mrs. Goodman. Your late husband and God."

"He loved our babies so much. I think he loved them more than I did. He was always saying that they made him proud, because they were ours, and *I* made him proud."

"You never know nobody completely," said Bonnie. "Take my husband. What he thinks about, it's a total mystery. Well, it is to me."

Mrs. Goodman unfolded a Kleenex and dabbed it against her cheeks. "My father always said that Aaron would come to no good. He said he was beneath me, I should have married a lawyer or a realtor, somebody professional, not a dry cleaner."

"Hey, you can't help who you fall in love with."

"I know. But why did he *do* it? I talked to him on the phone only about a half hour before it happened, and he sounded fine. He was talking about going to the reservoir Friday to do some fishing. You don't talk about fishing and then kill your children."

Bonnie took hold of her hand. "I can't even begin to understand why your late husband did what he did, Mrs. Goodman, but I can do my best to clean this place up for you so that you can go on living the rest of your life."

The tears began to slide down Mrs. Goodman's cheeks again, and this time she made no effort to wipe them away. "They were so beautiful. They were so, so beautiful. Little Benjamin, little Rachel, little Naomi."

Bonnie waited for a decent period while Mrs. Goodman silently wept. Eventually she glanced at her watch. "Mrs. Goodman, most people don't realize that the police don't do the cleaning up after a tragedy like this. You have to call in a specialist cleaner like me and pay for it yourself. Now I'm not the only cleaner available. I'll give you an estimate, but you're welcome to look in the Yellow Pages if you think my prices are too high."

Mrs. Goodman frowned at her as if she were speaking Greek.

"Do you have insurance, Mrs. Goodman?" Bonnie persisted. "I'm sorry to sound so businesslike, but a cleaning job like this could run you into quite a lot of expense."

"Insurance?"

"You should listen to her, Mrs. Goodman," Dan put in. "This lady knows what she's talking about."

"Right now, Mrs. Goodman, you're at your most vulnerable," Bonnie told her. "You're going to have all kinds of sharks circling. People offering to clean your house, sort out your legal problems, restructure your finances. All I'm trying to do is protect your interests here."

"Aaron never cared about money. If he had it, he spent it."

"I'm sure. But this job could cost upward of fifteen-hundred dollars, not to mention replacement rugs and furniture. You're probably okay. Most regular insurance policies also cover trauma-loss restoration. If you give me the name of your insurance agent, I'll talk to him this afternoon—see if you're entitled to put in a claim."

"Insurance agent? I don't know. Aaron handled all of that."

"Well, no need to stampede. Here's my card. As soon as you find out who he is, give me a call."

"You can do it, though? You can clean it all up? You can make it look the way it was before?"

"Pretty much, Mrs. Goodman, yes."

"You can't make my life look the way it was, though, can you?"

"No, Mrs. Goodman, I can't do that."

Mrs. Goodman gave Bonnie's hand a tighter squeeze. Her fingers were very cold, and it was like being gripped by a corpse. "Will you call me Bernice?"

"Bernice? For sure, if that's what you want."

*   *   *

Just as Bonnie was leaving the Goodman house, a thirtyish man in a flax summer-weight suit walked in, followed by a Mexican girl of about seventeen, wearing a dark blue sleeveless dress with big black flowers on it. The man was an inch shorter than Bonnie, with crinkly ginger hair and rimless glasses. The girl was moonfaced and plain, with pockmarked cheeks and pigtails.

"Help you?" Dan asked him.

"Dean Willits, friend of the family. I've come for Mrs. Goodman. And Consuela here needs to pick up some clothes."

"Ah, yes. Mrs. Goodman is right through there, in the kitchen. I'll have an officer accompany Consuela."

Dean Willits looked around the living room. "Holy shit," he said, when he saw the shotgun blast in the plaster and the fountain of blood up the wall. "I didn't have any idea."

"Let's just get Mrs. Goodman out of here, shall we?" Dan prompted him.

"Yeah, sure. Sorry. Aaron was such a great friend of mine, that's all. A terrific father, you know? A really outstanding father. Wouldn't touch a hair on those kids' heads."

"Yes, well," said Dan.

Outside, in the glare of the midday sunshine, Dan said, "I'll leave it with you, then?"

"You bet," said Bonnie.

"Something bothering you?"

"No, not really. I was wondering the same thing

that Mrs. Goodman was wondering. A terrific father who loved his children so much. What the hell possessed him to *kill* them?"

Dan shook his head. "Cases like these, you never find out."

Bonnie ducked under the police tape and walked back to her car. Dan followed her and opened the door for her. It groaned on its hinges like an irritated pig.

"How about I buy you dinner tomorrow night?"

"I'm not your type. Besides, what would I tell Duke?"

"You don't have to tell him anything. This is the age of sexual equality."

"Bullshit. If this is the age of equality, what am I doing running two jobs while my husband is sitting at home watching TV?"

"You ought to stop for a moment, Bonnie. You ought to stop and smell the flowers."

"Sorry, Dan. I'm too busy cleaning up the smell of dead bodies."

"Cynic."

"Lecher."

Lunch Menu

She met her friend Susan Spang at the Green Rainbow on the corner of Sunset and Alta Loma. It took her more than fifteen minutes to decide what she ought to eat, while Susan impatiently played with her fork. At last she chose:

Warm red cabbage salad with chorizo, green olives and goat cheese (674 calories)
Beef and tiny corn stir-fry with pepper confetti (523 calories)
Grilled figs (311 calories)
Evian water (0 calories)

THE MEANING OF HUMAN TRAGEDY

She had known Susan since high school. In those days they had been the closest of friends, sisters almost, and they had both fantasized that they would be movie stars. They had even cut stars out of baking foil, written their names on them and stuck them to the sidewalk on Hollywood Boulevard. Bonnie would be called "Sabrina Golightly," and Susan would be called "Tunis Velvet." Now they met only three or four times a year, and they hardly had anything to say to each other, but Bonnie was reluctant to end their friendship altogether. It would be like finally admitting that her teenage dreams would never come true and that she would never own a million-dollar diamond ring or a pink house in Bel Air. Apart from that, Susan was the only friend she had who didn't talk about shopping or children or what to do with leftover chicken.

Susan was tall and intense, with glossy black hair that reached all the way down to her waist and a pale, starved-looking face with enormous black eyes. Today she was wearing a short purple dress embroidered with silver stars and a big, floppy felt hat that looked as if a medieval dwarf were perched on her head.

She was sitting at a table in the corner with her long legs crossed underneath it.

"You look ex-*hausted*," was the first thing she said.

"Thanks. I am."

"Can you not scrape your chair? I have one of my headaches."

"Sorry. You should have canceled."

"I didn't want to cancel. I wanted to see you. I'm so tired of people who aren't real."

"Well, I'm glad I'm *real*."

"You are. That's the point. You're completely real. You always have been. I don't know how you've managed to stay so real."

"I don't know either."

A Chinese-American waiter in a long green apron came up to their table and recited the day's specials.

"*Sangchi ssam*, what's that?" Susan interrupted.

"It's a dish inspired by Korean cuisine. Highly seasoned ground beef and tofu in a parcel of radicchio, topped with mint and chili sauce."

Bonnie thought: Give me a double cheese-and-bacon burger any day. But this time it had been Susan's choice of restaurant.

Susan swallowed an ibuprofen tablet and half a

glass of Evian water. "I can't drink Perrier anymore. It reminds me too much of Clive."

"How is Clive?"

"Oh, he's still with that synthetic-chested teenager. You should see him. No, you shouldn't see him. He's dyed his hair blond. He looks like an alien. Well, he always did."

"Duke's okay," Bonnie volunteered.

"And Ray? I'll bet he's eight feet tall by now. Does he still want to be a WWF wrestler?"

Bonnie smiled and shook her head. She suddenly felt that time was passing her by.

"And how's *business*?" asked Susan, pulling a ghoulish face.

"It's okay, yes, ticking over good. We have a natural death to clean up tomorrow and two suicides Friday. The natural should be something. The guy died in the hot tub, and they didn't find him for seven-and-a-half weeks. It was only when his body fat blocked up the drain."

"My God, Bonnie, I don't know how you do it. I really don't. I think I'd—I don't know what I'd do. Barf. Faint. Barf and faint, both."

"Somebody has to do it. The police won't do it and the coroner's department won't do it and the county won't do it. It's a public service, that's all."

"I can't even think about it. The *smell*. A coyote died in our crawl space once."

Bonnie shrugged. "Blob of Vicks on your upper lip—that's all you need."

Susan shivered.

*　　*　　*

While they were eating, Bonnie's cell phone rang. It was Dean Willits, calling for Bernice Goodman. He was driving along the Ventura Freeway, so his voice kept breaking up. "I've talked to Mrs. Goodman's insurance agent, and he says fine, go ahead and clean up. Guy called Frears, says he knows you."

"That's great, Mr. Willits. I should be able to get there tomorrow afternoon."

"Frears has the keys, okay?"

Bonnie went back to her stir-fry. She put a forkful of beef and baby corn into her mouth and started to chew, but it was tepid and greasy and underdone and she suddenly thought of the children's beds with the bloody, blown-apart comforters, and she couldn't swallow it. At last she retched and spat it out into her napkin.

"What's the matter?" Susan asked her. "Bonnie— you've gone so *white*."

"It was something I saw this morning, that's all. You don't want to hear about it while you're eating."

"For goodness' sake, tell me. What are friends for?"

Bonnie described the Goodman house. Susan sat and listened and nodded.

"So that's it," said Bonnie. "I don't know why it's affected me more than any other trauma scene I've been to. Maybe I felt the same way as Mrs. Goodman . . . like the children were still there, you know? Or at least their souls were."

"You really felt their souls?"

"I don't know. . . . I felt something. Like there was somebody there, but there wasn't. It was scary. Very depressing."

"You felt their souls. That's wonderful! Do you know what that is?"

"Sorry? I don't understand you."

"That's Gilgul, the transmigration of souls. To be able to *feel* it, that shows that you're very receptive. You really ought to come see my kabbalah instructor. His name's Eitan Yardani, and he's so enlightening. Like your whole life will be so *fulfilled*."

"Susan, what are you talking about?"

"The kabbalah, of course. Everybody's into it. Madonna, Elizabeth Taylor. It shows you how to find all the answers to your inner self. It's like there's one God, En Sof, so far away from human thought that some kabbalists call it Ayin, the Nothingness."

"But the kabbalah—that's Jewish, isn't it? I'm a Catholic."

"So what? Is Madonna Jewish? Am I? So long as you find the infinite truth, what does it matter what religion you are? The kabbalah teaches us that everything in life has a special meaning, even if it's hidden. Those children died for a reason, Bonnie; and you could look through the texts and find out what it is."

"I don't think I *want* to find out what it is."

"You felt them, Bonnie! You felt their presence! That's totally kabbalistic. You may not want to find out—but what if they want to tell you?"

Bonnie couldn't think what to say. If Susan hadn't been her lifelong friend, she would have dropped her fork and walked out. She was used to Susan's spiritual flirtations. Last month she wouldn't stop enthusing about the Dalai Lama, and in the spring it was Sufi. But as far as Bonnie was concerned, Benjamin, Rachel and Naomi had been murdered less than twenty-four hours ago, and their deaths couldn't be explained by the kabbalah, or the Tarot, or anything else but the plain factual truth, no matter how hideous that truth might be. Their father had gone crazy and shot them. That was all.

"Do you know what you ought to do, Susan?" she interrupted. "You ought to come along with me one day, when we're clearing up a trauma scene. You wouldn't believe that human beings contain so much blood."

"I told you, I'd throw up."

"Maybe you would. But you'd look infinity right in the eye, and I think you'd forget your kabbalah."

"You're trying to make fun of me."

"I'm not," said Bonnie, pushing her plate away. "I'm sorry. I shouldn't have told you any of this. It wasn't fair."

Susan fiercely prodded her raw tuna salad. "You've changed. Do you know that? You never used to be so cynical."

"I'm sorry. I've said I'm sorry."

"I was only trying to help you, Bonnie. I was only trying to show you that life has its affirmative side, too. I mean, you're so negative these days."

"What?" said Bonnie.

"I can't—I don't know. It's like you're somebody else."

"I don't understand you. What do you mean I'm like somebody else?"

"You were always laughing. You were always like—I don't know. Sunshine."

Bonnie found herself worriedly scratching at her forearm. "I still laugh." Although she thought, *When? When was the last time I really laughed?*

"I don't want to hurt you, Bonnie. But it's *depressing.*"

"You think I'm depressing?"

Susan pressed the palms of both hands flat on the

table and stared Bonnie directly in the eye. Her breath came in small, compressed sniffs. "I'll tell you something, Bonnie. I'm positive for life. It's taken me years to find life. And when I say life, I'm talking about creation, and fulfillment, and transformation."

"Yes? I know that. Who isn't? What do you want me to say?"

Susan opened her mouth and closed it again without saying anything. She was so upset that she was hyperventilating. "It's just that—you're all about death. You walked into the restaurant, and I could feel it. You carry death around with you like a—like you're *wearing* it. Like a black veil, Bonnie. And I can't take it. I'm sorry, but I have to tell you how I feel. It frightens me and it brings me down."

"So? You don't want to see me anymore? Is that what you're saying?"

Susan was in a mess of tears. She gave an airy wave of her hand, and then she pressed her knuckles against her mouth.

"Listen, Susan, if you don't want to see me anymore, then you only have to say so. If I'm death incarnate—you know—I don't want to cast a shadow over your spiritual affirmation or anything. God forbid. Or En Sof forbid. Or whatever."

The waiter came up. "Is everything all right?" he asked, staring uneasily at their scarcely touched food.

Susan took a tiny tissue out of her diminutive pocketbook and wiped her nose. She wouldn't even look at Bonnie. "I'll take care of this," she said, offering her platinum card.

"I'm death, am I?" said Bonnie, as they waited for the check. "You really think I'm death?"

"I'm sorry, Bonnie. I have a headache. You were right. I should have canceled."

She stood up, but Bonnie took hold of her sleeve. "Are we going to see each other again?"

Susan whispered, "Sure," but Bonnie knew that she was lying. She stayed at the table and watched her go. The last time she saw her was when she was crossing Sunset, flicking her hair back with her hand. A last frozen Polaroid. And to think of all the days and all the nights; all the parties and all the bus trips; all the laughter and all the teenage despair. They had kissed each other once, on the pier at Venice Beach, at sunset, with the gulls screaming, because they loved each other. Love, ageless and evergreen, seldom seen by two.

The waiter came up. "You want anything else, ma'am?"

"No, thank you," said Bonnie. "What I need, you don't have here."

She stopped halfway along Hollywood Boulevard, double-parked, and went into the Super Star Grill. It was noisy inside, all tiles and chrome and Meatloaf screaming "Bat Out Of Hell." She bought a giant chili dog with onions and kraut and sat in the car and messily devoured it, watching her eyes in the rearview mirror as she did so.

So this is what death looks like. A thirty-four-year-old blonde with chili round her mouth. She finished the hot dog and drove away with sticky hands. She hadn't even driven as far as Vine Street before her vision was blurred with tears.

DUKE APOLOGIZES

Duke had bought her a dozen red roses, which lay wilting on the kitchen table. He came in from the yard still blowing out cigarette smoke. She didn't like him smoking in the house. He was wearing a faded black T-shirt with a Harley Davidson emblem on it.

"Hey, look, I'm sorry," he said.

She put down her shopping bags. "What are you sorry for? Everybody has off days once in a while."

"The Mexican chicken thing. That was—"

"Insane? Yes, it was. But that was yesterday and this is today and thank you for the flowers. How much did they sting you for them?"

Duke shrugged and looked sheepish. "They were— well, I got them for not very much."

"How much is not very much?"

"I got them for free, okay?"

She picked them up. "You got a dozen red roses for nothing? What did you do, take them off somebody's grave?"

"Rita at the florist. You know Rita. I told her what happened, and she kind of took pity on me."

"Oh, so now *Rita* knows that we had a fight about Mexican chicken? Who else did you tell? Jimmy down at the TV repair shop? Karen at the beauty parlor? I suppose the next time I go to the market they're all going to be clucking at me and singing 'La Cucaracha'?"

Duke banged his fist on the draining board. "Why do you always have to be so goddamn funny? Why don't you ever listen to anything I ever say without making a goddamn comedy act out of it? I brought you some roses, right, because I wanted to tell you that I was sorry about yesterday, right? I brought you some roses because I meant it. And what do I get? 'Did you take them off somebody's goddamn grave?'"

Bonnie carefully laid the roses back on the table. It was way past seven, and she should have been starting the evening meal.

"This time yesterday," she said, "three young children were getting themselves ready for bed."

"What?" said Duke. He was totally baffled. "What children?"

"One was nine and one was seven and one was only four. I even know what their names were."

"So—so what? What the hell are you talking about?"

She glanced up at the kitchen clock. "That was yesterday. Today they're dead."

"What?" said Duke. Bonnie came up to him and wrapped her arms around him and hugged him tight. "Hey, I can't breathe here."

"You don't have to be sorry and bring me flowers or anything. It's me. I don't know what's happening to me."

"You work too frigging hard, that's all. Why don't you give up this cleaning thing? It's not a nice thing to do, you know. I know it brings in the shekels, but we could sell the truck and make a few bucks, right? And I'll tell you what I'll do. I'll get myself a job, right? I will, I solemnly swear to God. Doesn't matter what it is. Dog walking, anything. I swear to God."

"You hate dogs."

"They're okay. Just because that Schnauzer took a hunk out of my ass."

Bonnie laughed. It was the first time that she had really laughed all day.

THE NEXT MORNING

She stood naked on the bathroom scales and stared at herself in the mirror.

Height 5 ft 4½ inches
Target weight 132 lbs
Actual weight 147 lbs

Ray knocked on the door. "Come on, Mom. I'm going to miss the bus."

"I'll drive you," she said. She needed to look at herself a few minutes longer, as if to reassure herself that she wasn't going to vanish.

CLEANING UP

That morning she had two of her three part-time assistants to help her, Ruth and Esmeralda. Jodie had scalded her arm and had to take two weeks off. Ruth was wearing a bright cerise track suit, her hair tied back with a yellow chiffon scarf. Esmeralda was a plump, solemn Mexican woman with dark-rimmed eyes, as if she hadn't slept in a month. Today, as usual, she wore black, with black lace-up shoes that monotonously squeaked on the kitchen floor.

Between them they rolled up the living room carpet. They had to lift the couch over it, and the couch weighed so much that it left them gasping.

"I'm getting too old for this," said Ruth.

"You should exercise more. Why don't you join my t'ai-chi ch'uon class?"

"Because I'd never go to it, just like *you* never go to it."

"I went last week. Well, maybe the week before. It's so hard to find the time, that's all. My life seems to be so—*filled up*."

In an oddly uneasy voice, Esmeralda said, "That stain has gone right through to the floorboards."

Bonnie came over and looked at it. Aaron Goodman's blood had soaked right through the underlay and formed a wide brownish blotch, like a Rorschach test.

Bonnie said, "That's all right. It's oak. We can probably get most of it out if we scrub it with sodium perborate."

Esmeralda crossed herself. "I think it's better if I make a start on the wall."

"You're sure? This is nothing like so yukky."

"No, no. I do the wall."

"Is something wrong?" Bonnie asked her.

"My knee's bad. I can't do too much bending."

"You crossed yourself."

Esmeralda gave her a hollow, noncommunicative look. "A small gesture for the dead, that's all."

"Okay . . . you can do the floor then, Ruth. I'll start bagging up the bedcovers."

They worked for an hour and a half. Bonnie's steam cleaner hissed and whuffled in the bedrooms, while Ruth's vacuum cleaner droned around the rest of the apartment and Esmeralda's scrubbing brush set up a brisk, percussive rhythm on the walls.

Bonnie usually sang while she worked. "Love, ageless and evergreen . . ." But in Naomi's bedroom she was silent. She couldn't take her eyes away from the bloody stencil patterns that Naomi's hands had made across the wall, yet somehow she couldn't bring herself to clean them off. It would be almost like denying that Naomi's last few moments of pain and bewilderment had ever happened.

She found herself wondering what Naomi must have thought of her father, as she crawled across the floor. She couldn't bear to think that she might have cried out to him to help her.

Esmeralda came in with a cloth and a Dettox spray. "The wall's finished," she said. Without hesitation she sprayed the handprints and wiped them away.

Bonnie switched off her steam cleaner and it gurgled into silence. "You can start on the couch if you want to."

"She's keeping the couch?"

"That's a thousand-dollar couch, easy."

"I couldn't keep my couch if my husband killed himself all over it. Even if it was ten-thousand dollars. I would always feel that there was a dead man sitting there."

"Yes, well, I get that with Duke when the World Series is on."

The room was hot and humid now, and smelled strongly of damp carpet. Bonnie went to the window and opened it wide. On the windowsill stood a large, leafy fig plant in a terra-cotta pot, and she shifted it to one side in case the drapes blew against it and knocked it over. As she did so, something black dropped from one of its leaves—something that squirmed.

"Urgh!" she said, and jumped back.

"What's the matter?"

"It's some kind of maggot or something. It dropped off that plant."

Esmeralda came over and peered into the compost inside the pot. A fat black caterpillar was crawling up the stem of the plant, its body undulating as it climbed.

"That's disgusting," said Bonnie. "Look—there's more of them." Half concealed in the foliage were four or five more caterpillars, all of them steadily eating, so that the edges of the fig leaves were all serrated in tiny jagged patterns.

Esmeralda crossed herself again, twice.

"Why do you keep doing that?" Bonnie demanded.

"I hate these things. They come from the devil."

"They're caterpillars. They won't hurt you."

"I hate them, the black ones. They bring bad luck."

"You're so darn superstitious, Esmeralda. You're worse than Ruth. But if you don't like them, go get the permethrin spray and zap them. Anyways, I don't think that Mrs. Goodman would appreciate what they're doing to her fig."

Bonnie looked around the bedroom to make sure that she hadn't missed anything. Naomi's bed was completely stripped now, and later this afternoon she would come back to take the rest of it away. The bunk beds she would dismantle and take down to the American Humane Association's children's home.

A warm breeze stirred the nets and brushed them against the houseplant, and Bonnie's attention was drawn back to the caterpillars. She had seen just about every variety of bug and maggot since she had started cleaning up trauma scenes, but she had never seen anything like these before. Maybe the eggs had already been mixed up in the compost when Mrs. Goodman had bought it, and they had only just hatched out.

Esmeralda came in with the insecticide spray.

"Wait," said Bonnie. "I want to keep one of these. Maybe Dr. Jacobson can tell me what they are."

She tugged out a disposable plastic glove and blew into it. Then she held it under one of the caterpillars and shook the leaf on which it was perched. It clung tenaciously, but in the end she flipped at it with another glove and it dropped off into one of the fingers. She pulled off a few fragments of fig leaf and pushed those into the glove, too.

"Don't want it going hungry," she said.

Esmeralda wrinkled up her nose. "Why do you want to keep such a thing?"

"I'm curious. I'm a naturally inquisitive person, that's all."

"It's bad luck, that thing."

Esmeralda sprayed the fig plant backward and forward until Bonnie was almost choking with the fumes. One caterpillar began to writhe, and then another, and then one by one they dropped off onto the windowsill.

"I think you're enjoying this," said Bonnie.

"You want me to pretend that I'm not?" Esmeralda sprayed another caterpillar and said, "Die, you wriggly son of a bitch!"

Bonnie left her to it and went back through to the living room. They were practically all done now. With the help of a muscular young man they had recruited for ten dollars on the corner of Hollywood and Highland, they had already cut the Goodmans' carpet into three manageable sections and loaded it onto the back of Bonnie's truck. The walls were clean, although the hole from the shotgun blast remained untouched: Bonnie didn't redecorate, although she could refer people. The cream leather couch was clean, too, but it had lost its shine. The metallic smell of blood had been replaced by a mildly antiseptic tang, like that in a dentist's waiting room. Ruth had vacuum cleaned everywhere, although she hadn't polished. "We clean up, we sterilize, we don't do maid work."

Where Aaron Goodman's blood had spilled there was still the faintest phantom of a stain, but the only way to get rid of it completely would have been to pry up the floorboards.

Bonnie walked around the stain. She wasn't very happy about it. "This is really the best we can do?"

"It soaked right into the grain. I could have another try with a stronger solution, but I don't want to bleach out the wood."

Bonnie walked around and around, and she couldn't stop looking at the stain. She didn't know why. For some reason it disturbed her, like the words of a song that she couldn't quite remember, or a whispered warning. It was the shape, she supposed—like a huge pale flower, or a giant moth.

THAT EVENING

Bonnie arrived home that evening sweaty and light-headed with exhaustion. Apart from the Goodman home, she and Ruth had cleaned up a natural death scene in Westwood. A woman in her mid-eighties had died in her sleep and lain undiscovered for nine weeks. Her son had prowled up and down the hallway while they worked, a podgy, pale man with a jet-black hairpiece, constantly checking his watch. Bonnie had resisted the temptation to ask him why he hadn't called his mother in all that time.

"I live in Albuquerque," he had suddenly volunteered, as they were stacking away their plastic buckets.

Oh, really? Bonnie had thought, grim-faced. *And they don't have telephones in Albuquerque?* On the way home, she thought: *I should have shown him his moth-er's sheets.*

She went into the living room, where Duke was watching baseball. She kissed him on the top of his head, and he immediately ran his fingers through his hair to reerect his pompadour.

"How was your day, honey?" she asked him, perching herself on the arm of his chair.

"Okay, I guess. I called Vincent at the Century Plaza. He might have some bar work for me."

"That's great! What would you have to do, mix cocktails and stuff? One frozen daiquiri, coming up! Pina colada, madam?"

"Unh-hunh. It's fetching and carrying mainly."

Bonnie gave him another kiss. "It's a job, though, isn't it? It's a start."

"Sure, it's a start," he agreed, shifting his head sideways so that she didn't block his view of the television.

Bonnie washed up and changed into a flowery yellow dress and a big yellow bead necklace. Her lucky color. She went into the kitchen and took six pimply chicken thighs out of the fridge.

"Fried chicken okay?"

"With gravy?"

She thought about the bloodstain on the Goodmans' floor. "Yes, with gravy."

She sieved flour onto a large white plate and seasoned it with salt and pepper and chili powder. "Has Ray been back yet?" she asked.

"Ray? Not yet."

"Didn't he say he'd be late or nothing?"

"Didn't say nothing."

"Ralph wants me to go to Pasadena tomorrow."

"Pasadena? What the hell's in Pasadena?"

"Moist-Your-Eyes promotion."

"I suppose *he's* going, too? Mr. Wonderful?"

"What is it with you and Ralph? Why do you always act so jealous whenever it's anything to do with Ralph?"

"It's the way the guy looks at you. Don't tell me you haven't noticed it. Like he's mentally taking off your clothes."

Bonnie, with floury hands, went to the kitchen door. "Duke—once and for all—I am not interested in Ralph Kosherick. I have never been interested in Ralph Kosherick, and I never *will* be interested in Ralph Kosherick."

"You mention the guy's name three times in one sentence and you're not interested in him?"

Bonnie looked at her watch, then up at the kitchen clock. "Ray's so late. I wish he'd call."

"You can see it in his eyes. Unhooking your brassiere. Pulling down your panty hose with his teeth."

"Shut up, Duke. I'm not in the mood."

Ray didn't come home in time for supper, so they ate together in the living room and watched television, the way they used to when they first got married.

"It's good," said Duke, his eyes still fixed on the screen and gravy glistening on his chin.

When they had finished, Bonnie carried the empty chicken plates back into the kitchen and took a chocolate-fudge cake out of the fridge. She cut a large slice for Duke and another, slightly smaller slice for herself. She crammed almost all of the smaller slice into her mouth at once and ate it while she noisily scraped the chicken bones into the bin under the sink. By the time she returned to the living room she had finished it and wiped her mouth.

"You're not having none?" asked Duke.

"Are you kidding me? That's three hundred and thirty calories a *look*."

Duke shrugged and took a generous bite. "See this guy?" he said, nodding toward the television. "He ate an entire Volkswagen."

"What did he do that for?"

"How the hell should I know? Like, what do people eat chocolate cake for?"

Bonnie didn't answer, but she knew why *she* ate chocolate cake.

She was sleeping deeply when the door chimes rang. She sat up in bed, listening, not quite sure if she had been dreaming or not. But then they rang again. She nudged Duke with her elbow and hissed, "Duke! Duke, wake up! There's somebody at the door!"

Duke croaked like a frog and eventually propped himself up on one elbow. "What? What the hell time is it?"

"Three twenty-five."

"The *hell*?"

Bonnie climbed out of bed, dragged her robe from the back of the door and went out into the corridor.

It was then that she saw the flashing red-and-blue lights outside the house and she knew that something was badly wrong. *"Duke!"* she called. "Duke, it's the police!" She hurried to the front door.

Two uniformed police officers were standing outside: one Hispanic with a little mustache, one black. "You Mrs. Winter?" asked the black officer, shining his flashlight in her face.

"What's happened? It's Ray, isn't it? Tell me what's happened!"

"It's okay, Mrs. Winter. Your son's been hurt, but he's going to be fine. He's over at the hospital right now, and if you want to see him, we can take you there."

"Hurt? What do you mean, hurt?"

By now Duke had appeared from the bedroom wearing a short pink bathrobe and black knee-length socks. "What's going on here?" he wanted to know.

"Mr. Winter? Your son, Ray, has been hurt, sir. He's over at the hospital having treatment."

"What was it? Auto accident? The kid doesn't even drive!"

"No, sir. It seems like there was some kind of ethnic confrontation."

Duke pressed two fingers against his forehead as if he were having trouble working this out. "Ethnic confrontation? What's that in English? You're talking about a race riot here?"

"Not exactly a riot, Mr. Winter. But there was a racially motivated assault, yes."

"How many of them were there?"

"I'm sorry?"

"You've just told me my son has been the victim of a racially motivated assault. I'm just asking you how many of them were there."

"Around seventeen, all told. But your son wasn't—"

"Seventeen! There were seventeen blacks against just one white? Jesus Christ!"

"Mr. Winter, your son wasn't attacked by seventeen other people. Your son was involved in a fight in which at least seventeen people are known to have taken part. Eleven whites and six Hispanics. No African-Americans. All of them sustained injuries ranging from stab wounds to severe bruising. One of them may lose an eye. Three of them, including your son, are still in hospital."

Bonnie said, "Ray was fighting *Hispanics*? Is that what you're trying to tell us?"

The black officer took out his notebook and flipped it open. "Eleven white youths went into the X-cat-ik Pool Bar downtown and a fight ensued. We recovered three knives, a machete and a baseball bat. Unfortunately, none of the customers in the bar was willing to admit that they saw anything, although there doesn't seem to be any question that this was a racially motivated attack."

"No, there's some mistake here," said Bonnie. "Ray wouldn't get involved in a thing like that."

"I'm only telling you the facts, Mrs. Winter."

Duke started to bluster again, but Bonnie laid a hand on his arm to quiet him. "Tell me where he is," she said. "We'll make our own way there."

THE YOUNG HERO

They found Ray in a dull green room at the end of a long, echoing corridor. One of its fluorescent lights kept flickering and making a buzzing noise like a trapped blowfly.

Ray's head was wrapped in a white bandage that went right under his jaw. One of his arms was in plaster so that only the purple tips of his fingers were showing. Both of his eyes were swollen like plums, yellow and red, and his lips were huge, as if they were molded out of red rubber.

A Chinese intern with deeply nicotine-stained fingers was checking his blood pressure. "You're the parents?"

Bonnie nodded. She walked around Ray's bed and said, "Ray? What happened to you, baby?"

"A broken wrist, multiple contusions and abrasions, three cracked ribs, a chipped ankle bone, two broken toes and a mild concussion," said the intern, impassively. "It could have been worse."

"It could have been *worse*?" asked Duke.

"Sure. He was kicked several times in the abdomen. Could have ruptured his spleen. Somebody kicked him in the head, too, just behind the right ear. He's going to have a pretty big egg there for a day or two."

Bonnie sat down and took hold of Ray's hand. "Ray—what were you doing? You're not in a gang, are you? I was expecting you home for supper."

Duke said nothing at all but stood with his arms tightly folded, pulling that chewing-the-cud face he always pulled when he couldn't trust himself to speak.

"I'm sorry, Mom," Ray croaked. "We didn't think it was going to turn out this way."

"But what were you thinking of, going down to that bar?"

"That's where all the Mexican kids hang out."

"So? What did they ever do to you? For God's sake, Ray, the police said you had knives and baseball bats."

"They were Mexicans, Mom."

"So they were Mexicans. So what? I don't get it. Why did you have to beat up on them like that?"

"Because of what they did, Mom."

"You'll have to excuse my stupidity. I still don't get it."

"Because of what they did to Dad, Mom. Because they come here and take American jobs and put people out of work."

"You went and beat up on some Mexicans you didn't even know because some Mexican took your father's job?"

"Yes," said Ray, and coughed, and winced. "I mean, look what it's done to you, Mom, both of you. Dad's all eaten up inside, and you have to scrape up dead bodies for a living, and you two are always having arguments, and it's all because of some Mexican."

Bonnie shook her head in disbelief. "What were you thinking? You could have killed somebody and spent the rest of your life in jail! Somebody might have killed *you*! Look at you! They almost succeeded!"

She stood up. She was quaking with rage. "You're my son, Ray. You're my only son. I brought you up to do the right thing. Your father lost his job, and that was unfair, and it was probably illegal, too. But for you to start beating up on Mexican people like some kind of Nazi—I won't have that. No son of mine is going to behave like that, I warn you."

Duke took hold of her arm and tried to restrain her. "Come on, Bonnie. Look at him. Don't you think he's been punished enough?"

"Are you serious? Your son went out armed with knives and baseball bats and deliberately attacked innocent people!"

"Hey, hey, let's hold up a minute, shall we? You say innocent. But how the hell do you know they're innocent? These Mexicans, they take work without permits, they don't pay taxes, they deal in drugs, they smuggle stuff. They'd sell their own sisters, most of them. How can you say innocent? And in any case, tell me, how do we know for sure who attacked who?"

Bonnie turned around and stared at him. "I can't believe I'm hearing this."

"You have to be fair, sweetheart. You can't shout at the kid without knowing all the details."

"*Fair?* I know what this is all about. You're proud of him, aren't you? You're actually proud of him. You think he's some kind of hero. You didn't ever think that he'd take your side, did you? But now he has, and you're so goddamned *proud*!"

"Hey, come on, Bonnie—"

"Forget it, Duke. I'm going home. I'm not staying here to listen to this bigoted crap. Ray—did the cops talk to you yet?"

Ray dumbly shook his head.

"Well, don't say a word to nobody. Not to the cops, not to the doctors, not to nobody. Wait till I can talk to some friends of mine downtown. I'm supposed to go to Pasadena in the morning, but I'll cancel. Don't say a single word—you understand me? And don't forget to tell the nurses that you're allergic to broccoli."

Ray turned his face away. Bonnie could see that he wasn't ready to say that he was sorry, not yet. His father gave him a grunt and a pat on the shoulder and then followed Bonnie out of the room and along the echoing corridor.

In the elevator, Duke said, "Jesus, Bonnie. That's what America was built on: people fighting for what they believed in. People don't do that anymore. All these goddamned ethnic minorities. Dave Guthrie just lost his job at the bakery to some greaser. Why don't the Mexicans just come around to our houses and take our furniture?"

"All right, Davy Crockett," said Bonnie. "I've had enough for one night."

WHAT RALPH SAID

"If you don't make this trip to Pasadena, Bonnie, then I'm real sorry, but I'm going to have to find somebody more reliable. You hear what I'm saying?"

"You mean you'll fire me?"

"I need somebody I can count on, Bonnie, one-hundred percent."

"Ralph, will you have a heart? Ray's all beaten up and the police could be charging him with assault with a deadly weapon."

"I understand, Bonnie. I truly understand. But this trip could make the difference between profit and loss."

"I can't do it, Ralph. If you feel you have to fire me, then fire me. My family comes first."

Ralph was silent for a while. Then he said, "I'm very disappointed, Bonnie. You don't even know how much."

WHAT SHE TOOK TO THE HOSPITAL

She stopped at the ministore before she went to see Ray in the hospital and bought him:

Three peaches
One giant-size bottle of Dr Pepper
Rainbow Chips Deluxe
One Colgate toothbrush with flexible head
One tube Arm & Hammer toothpaste
One box menthol Kleenex
One copy *Soap Opera Digest*

LORD OF THE FLIES

Bonnie spent nearly an hour at Ray's bedside that morning. His face was still swollen and his bruises had turned purple, but he had recovered from his concussion and he was much more lively.

He watched television, snorting at *Rugrats* while Bonnie made calls to the police department, trying to find out which officers had attended the fracas at the X-cat-ik Pool Bar and how likely they were to press charges.

"Do you mind turning that down?" she asked Ray, with one finger pressed in her ear.

"What?" he said.

"Down. The volume. I'm trying to get you out of trouble here."

In the end, with her mobile phone beeping *recharge* at her, she managed to talk to Captain O'Hagan.

Captain O'Hagan said nothing much except "mmh-

hmmh" and "right" and "right," but in the end he
said, "I can't make you any promises, Bonnie. But
I'll take a look at the charge sheet and see if I can
do a little origami with it."

"I owe you one, Dermot."

"Not yet you don't. But if you do, you can bet
your sweet buns that I'll collect on it."

She snapped the phone cover shut and said,
"That's it, Ray. You're in with a chance, anyhow."

"Thanks, Mom. Outstanding. Is Dad coming to
see me?"

"He said he would. But he has to go for a job
interview this morning. Bar work, over at the Century Plaza."

"You're kidding."

Bonnie gave a wry smile. She stood up and
watched Ray for a while, while he watched television. *You think you know your children. You think
they're you.* But of course Ray was Duke as well. In
fact, he was more like Duke than she had ever realized. She kissed him gently and precisely on the
cheek and then she left. He didn't say anything, not
even "good-bye."

She drove up to UCLA. The morning was already
very warm, and she opened all the car windows.
When she stopped at the traffic signals at the inter-
section of Wilshire and Beverly Glen, a gold Mercedes convertible drew up close alongside her, driven
by a fiftyish man with wraparound dark glasses and
a bald head mottled with sunburn.

"Hey, honey!" he called out. "You're a road haz-
ard—did you know that?"

She looked in the other direction. She knew that there was a long section of trim flapping loose from the Electra's offside door, and whenever she put her foot on the gas a cloud of blue smoke billowed out, but apart from that the car was running not bad.

When she didn't respond, the man leaned across his seat and said, "I can't keep my eyes off you—that's why!"

The signals changed to green and she pulled away with a squeal of tires and a deafening backfire, which flustered her even more. The Mercedes kept pace with her for a while, the man grinning at her with unnaturally white teeth, but just before they reached UCLA he gave her a toot on his horn and turned off toward Bel Air.

When he was out of sight, she looked at herself in the rearview mirror. The woman who looked back at her was as much of a stranger as Ray.

Dr. Jacobson's laboratory was in a prefabricated cedar-wood building at the back of the main science block. Bonnie parked directly outside, at an angle, and a mourning dove was calling sadly in the trees as she climbed up the wooden steps. A small sign said DEPARTMENT OF ENTOMOLOGY. PLEASE CLOSE ALL DOORS.

Bonnie had to push her way through three sets of finely meshed screen doors, which slammed behind her one by one. Inside the laboratory it was uncomfortably humid and smelled of dead vegetation. The walls were lined with glass vivaria of insects—stick insects and praying mantises and locusts and fat white grubs—as well as dozens of cases of dead butterflies and moths. There were also diagrams of insect life cycles and hugely magnified photographs of flies and larvae.

A young girl with very long dark hair and large circular glasses was bent over a workbench in the center of the laboratory. She was carefully squeezing something from an eye dropper into a cardboard box. Bonnie came up to her and peered inside, and then wished she hadn't. Crouched in the bottom of the box was the largest, hairiest spider she had ever seen. It was trembling, as if it were just about ready to strike. "What do you call that?" she asked, wrinkling up her nose.

"Chelsea," the girl told her, without looking up.

"Pretty unusual name for a spider."

"I don't know. It's more personal than *aphonopelma*."

"Is Dr. Jacobson here? I was supposed to meet him at ten-thirty but I'm running late."

"He's in back. Go right on through."

Howard Jacobson was sitting in a small sunlit office in front of a Fujitsu PC, furiously hammering at the keys. He was tall and angular with bulging blue eyes and tufty black hair. As soon as Bonnie came in, he jumped up like a jack-in-the-box. "Bon-*neee!* Come on in! Great to see you! How would you like some coffee?"

"Sure, that'd be welcome."

"How's my favorite trauma-scene cleaner? I haven't seen you since that ax thing, have I? Jesus, the blood! The guts! Ugh-a-rugh-a! I don't know how you had the stomach to mop that up."

Bonnie moved a stack of computer printouts and sat herself down and covered her eyes with her hand.

"Are you okay?" Howard frowned.

"I've had a couple of problems at home, that's all. My son's in the hospital. Nothing life threatening, but it's bad enough."

"Flu?"

"Fight."

"That's too bad. But boys will be boys, huh? I was always getting into fights when I was younger. The other kids called me Bug Boy and used to sit on my head and fart in my ear. Amazing I can still hear."

"I just lost my job at Glamorex, too. Well, maybe not. I'll just have to see."

Howard handed her a mug of coffee. On the side it said, *Never ask yourself questions you don't know the answer to.*

"I'm not interrupting you?" she asked.

"Of course not. I'm polishing my latest paper, that's all. 'New Techniques for Determining Time of Death from Sarcophagidae Larvae Invasion.' Read it first, eat lunch afterward. Unless you're deliberately trying to lose weight, that is. You been busy?"

"Pretty much. People keep on killing each other. Somebody has to clean up after them."

"You said on the phone you had something interesting to show me."

"I don't know. Maybe it's nothing. I never saw one before, that's all."

Bonnie handed Howard a brown paper bag. He moved his keyboard to one side and carefully tipped the contents onto his desk—a scattering of fig-leaf fragments and the black caterpillar that she had found at the Goodman home. The caterpillar began to hump its way slowly across a sheet of graph paper. Howard leaned forward and peered at it from only inches away. Then he took a pair of half-glasses out of his desk, perched them on the end of his nose and peered at it even closer.

Bonnie said, "I almost didn't bring it—you know, what with Ray being in the hospital and all. But I thought I'd better in case it died."

"Sure, sure. I'm very glad you did. Where did you say you found it?"

"On a fig plant. There were maybe six or seven of them. You must have seen that shooting on TV—the guy on De Longpre who shot his three children and then blew his head off? The fig plant was on the windowsill in one of the bedrooms."

Howard nudged the caterpillar with his fingertip to prevent it from crawling under his computer console. "Now, you're a *very* unusual little guy, aren't you?"

"I don't know whether it has any direct connection to the trauma," said Bonnie. "But a couple of days ago I found some black chrysalis-type things at another trauma scene, and I just thought—you know—this is kind of weird."

"You didn't keep a sample of the chrysalis-type things?"

Bonnie shook her head. "I couldn't even tell you if they were the same kind of bug. But I just thought—you know—this is kind of weird."

"It *is* kind of weird, Bonnie. It's *highly* weird. This looks like *Parnassius mnemonsyne*, the Clouded Apollo. It's a large butterfly with white, black-veined wings with black spots. The dark, shadowy form occurs only in the females. . . . With age, the wings of the males become almost transparent.

"The interesting thing is that *Parnassius mnemonsyne* is found in only two places in the world: in the mountain pastures of Western Europe and in the hills of Chichimec territory in northern Mexico. Nobody knows for sure how this one butterfly could have developed in two such disparate locations. But there's no doubt that it was the same butterfly. I have some samples outside, if you want to take a look."

"No, thanks," said Bonnie. "Just tell me why this caterpillar should have been crawling around some trauma scene."

"I don't know. I mean, the Clouded Apollo has something of a sinister reputation in Aztec culture, but that's superstition, nothing else."

"What reputation?"

Howard Jacobson frowned at her and said, "You're serious, aren't you? You don't think that this larva could have had anything to do with your trauma scene?"

"I don't know. Not really. It was so tragic, that's all. I can't understand how a loving father could have murdered his children like that."

"Well, I'm not a psychologist. I'm still just a bug boy."

"What reputation?"

"It's a legend, Bonnie. Forget it."

"*What* reputation?"

"Okay . . . the Clouded Apollo butterfly was supposed to be the daytime disguise of an Aztec demon called Itzpapalotl. She was the most dreaded of all

Aztec demons, a combination of insect and monster. She had butterfly wings edged all around with obsidian knives, and her tongue was a sacrificial knife, too.

"Sometimes she wore magic clothes—a *naualli* or cloak that enabled her to transform herself into an innocent-looking butterfly.

"She was the patroness of witches and hideous human sacrifices. She presided over the thirteen unlucky signs of the Aztec calendar. On those days she used to fly through towns and forests at the head of an army of dead witches, all returned from the underworld in the shape of butterflies."

"And what? What did she do?"

"She drove people mad so that they killed the people they loved the most."

Bonnie stared down at her cup of coffee as if she didn't know what it was.

"Cookie?" asked Howard. "I have some terrific pecan crunch."

THE WILD AND THE WAYWARD

Around 11:30 she drove to Lincoln Boulevard in Santa Monica to give a quotation on a suicide pact. She was supposed to meet the family lawyer outside the house, but he called her almost as soon as she drew up to the curb to say that he was delayed. He had one of those voices that sounded as if he were wearing a swimmer's nose clip.

"Delayed?" asked Bonnie. "How long?"

"I can be there in twenty minutes."

"Okay. But if it's twenty-one minutes I won't be here. If it's twenty-and-a-*half* minutes I won't be here."

She sat in the car listening to country music and tapping her fingers on the steering wheel. She wondered if she ought to visit her mother. She always felt guilty about her mother even if she visited her twice a week. Bonnie always felt that there was an unspoken question between herself and her mother—a question that was never answered—and the trouble was, she didn't even know what it was. Their relationship was like one of those cryptic crosswords that don't give you any clue numbers.

She dialed her mother's number, but she pressed the clear button as soon as her mother snapped, "Hello?" It would be better if she visited her by surprise. It would be even better if she didn't visit her at all. No, it wouldn't. She had to.

The house where the suicide pact had taken place stood on a corner plot of the 500 block—a two-story frame building with peeling white paint. It was deeply overshadowed on one side by a tall cedar tree, which gave it an almost unearthly gloom, and it had all the telltale signs of recent tragedy. An untended lawn, sagging drapes, and a Ralph's supermarket cart tipped over by the front door.

Not only that, but two of the upstairs windows were boarded up, and there was a smoke smudge just above the left-hand window, shaped like a waving black chiffon scarf. Bonnie didn't know the full details, but Lieutenant Munoz had told her that a forty-seven-year-old widow had been having an affair with her fifteen-year-old nephew. When her brother found out, he had called the police and threatened to have her prosecuted for child abuse. The same night the widow and the boy had lain on her four-poster bed together and doused themselves with three-and-a-half gallons of premium-grade gasoline. Clinging tightly together, they had set themselves alight.

There is never anything romantic about burning alive. The boy had leaped up from the bed and rushed around the room screaming in agony, setting fire to the drapes. Then he had run downstairs and tried to get out of the house by the front door. His fingers, however, were already too charred to draw back the safety chain and turn the handle. His body was found by the fire department still standing against the door, stuck to the paint like a grinning, shriveled monkey. The widow's body had been so badly burned that they couldn't decide which was mattress ash and which was human cinders. The contents of her funeral urn had been part widow and part Sealy.

Bonnie checked her watch. If the family lawyer didn't show up within four minutes exactly, she was leaving. She was sweltering, and she was feeling so hungry that she was nauseated.

She had already started her engine when a shiny red Porsche convertible drew up on the other side of the street, and a tall, suntanned man climbed out of it, wearing a cream polo shirt and white tennis shorts and carrying two racquets under his arm. He had well-cropped blond hair, mirror sunglasses and a strong cleft chin. He reminded her of somebody, but she couldn't think who it was.

He was about to walk toward the house opposite, but then he stopped and lifted his sunglasses and frowned at her. He came across the street and said, "Pardon me. Can I help you with something?"

"I'm fine, thanks."

He laid his hand on the door of her Electra. His

arm was very brown, with fine golden hairs and a
fine golden Rolex.

"You know what happened here?" he asked her.
She was absolutely sure that she had met him before.
But when did she ever get to meet men who looked
like this? She averted her eyes, but then she found
herself looking at his firm, suntanned thighs, and the
bulge in his crisp white tennis shorts. Immediately,
she lifted her head again and looked at herself in
his reflecting lenses—two of her, both plump, both
distorted, both perspiring.

"I know what happened here, sure."

"Well, we've had quite a few people driving by to
take a look at the place, and we've even had people
getting out of their cars and peering into the windows and having their photographs taken on the
front lawn. One family even brought a picnic. I'll tell
you. Can you believe that? Cold barbecued chicken
legs."

"And you think that's what I'm doing? Rubber-
necking?"

"I'm just telling you that what happened here was
a terrible human tragedy, and we'd prefer it if people
behaved with a little more respect."

"I see."

"So"—he made a sweeping gesture with his
hand—"if you don't mind being on your way."

She suddenly realized why she recognized him.
"You're Kyle Lennox!" she said, breathlessly. "That's
who you are! You're Kyle Lennox. From *The Wild and
the Wayward*!"

"Yes, I'm Kyle Lennox from *The Wild and the Way-*

ward, but that doesn't alter anything. This is where I live, and me and my neighbors are all pretty much sickened by people like you coming to . . . *ogle* this house. I knew Mrs. Marrin. She was a personal friend of mine. I knew her nephew, too. What do you think you're going to see here? An action replay?"

"No, no." Bonnie reached across to her glove compartment and took out one of her business cards. "That's what I'm doing here, Mr. Lennox. I'm waiting for the family lawyer so that I can give him a quotation for cleaning the house up."

Kyle Lennox lifted his sunglasses again and peered at the card with the palest blue eyes that Bonnie had ever seen. She had always thought he was handsome when she saw him on television, but to see him right here on the street. . . . She made a point of not looking down at his tennis shorts again.

"Hey, listen," he said. "I'm really sorry. I didn't have any idea."

"That's all right. When somebody dies in circumstances like these, it isn't surprising that their neighbors get kind of sensitive about it."

"No, I'm really sorry. I accused you of being a sicko and I was totally mistaken."

"It's all right, really. It was a pretty easy mistake to make."

"I didn't even know that there were special people—well, you know, I didn't know that there were special companies who cleaned up after suicides and stuff. Don't the cops do it?"

"They don't have the expertise. It takes more than a mop and a bucket to clean up after something like this."

"Jesus . . . I never knew. I'll bet you get to see some pretty gruesome things, huh?"

"Now and again. Mostly it's just stains."

"Jesus. How many trauma scenes do you go to every week?"

"Four, maybe. Sometimes more. People are always offing each other."

"Jesus. What was the worst one you ever saw?"

Bonnie pointed to her business card. "Would you mind signing that for me? I really love *The Wild and the Wayward*. Sign it for Duke, could you, my husband? He loves it, too. He watches it even more religious than me."

"Okay, sure. Do you have a pen?"

Bonnie took the chewed ballpoint pen from the top of her clipboard and handed it to him. He signed the card with a flourish. "There you go. *For Duke . . . You Too Can Be Wild and Wayward.*"

"Well, he can be pretty darn wayward. I'm not so sure about wild."

At that moment, a metallic-green Coupe de Ville arrived outside the house, and a small ginger-haired man climbed out. He shrugged on a wheat-colored sport coat and then raised his hand to Bonnie in greeting.

"That's the family lawyer?" asked Kyle Lennox.

"I guess," Bonnie nodded and climbed out of her car, too.

"I'd better leave you to it, then," said Kyle Lennox. "It's been real interesting to meet you, Bonnie . . . and sorry again about the misunderstanding. I hope you forgive me."

Bonnie smiled. "It's nothing, really. Forget it."

Until she stood beside him, she hadn't realized how tall he was—and how he smelled of suntanned, young, well-exercised man and Hugo aftershave by Hugo Boss. Forgive him? She would have forgiven him if he had publicly accused her of turning people's milk to vinegar and sleeping with Satan.

She watched him walk back across the street. She loved the little bounce in his step, a combination of fitness and very expensive tennis shoes. The family lawyer came up to her and stood beside her. "Isn't that—?"

"Yes, it is. He just gave me his autograph."

"My wife's going to be so sick when I tell her. I'm Dudley Freeberg, by the way. Freeberg, Treagus and Wolp."

"Nice to meet you, Mr. Freeberg."

"Well, likewise," said Dudley Freeberg, and gave her a gappy grin.

ASHES TO ASHES

Like all houses in which people have died violently, the Marrin residence was preternaturally silent, as if it were holding its breath at the horror of what had happened here.

But it was the stench of burned carpet that struck Bonnie the most. As she and Dudley Freeberg stepped into the hallway, their nostrils were filled with the fumy smell of gasoline, mixed with badly scorched wool. There was another smell, too, like those sour, charred fragments of hamburger that stick to the barbecue.

Dudley Freeberg peered around the back of the door, and then very cautiously closed it. On the inside, the white paint was bubbled and brown, and there was a sooty smoke trail all the way up to the ceiling. Ribbons of shriveled fabric hung from the upper part of the door, and the center panel had been scratched by a fan-shaped array of blunt, rectangular marks, as if somebody had been trying to scrape the paint off.

"Skin," said Bonnie, pointing to the fabric.

Dudley Freeberg took off his glasses and stared at it.

"*Skin?*" he said, and his Adam's apple went up and down.

"That's right. And those scrape marks are where the fire department had to detach his remains from the door. I can clean the organic remains okay and remove the smoke stains, but you'll have to bring in a professional painter to do the woodwork."

"I see," said Dudley Freeberg, in a hollow voice. "A professional painter."

They looked around the rest of the hallway in utter silence. It was large, high-ceilinged, decorated in lilacs and golds. A large pottery vase of long-dead gladioli stood on a mock-rococo side table, and there was a gilt-framed reproduction of a painting of two Mexicans in large sombreros sleeping in the sun. Through a half-open door Bonnie could see a spacious, limed-oak kitchen. She would have loved a house like this, even though it was shabby—a house with space and tasteful furnishings and a sweeping staircase.

It was the staircase that gave them the most vivid narrative of the last seconds of Mrs. Marrin's fifteen-year-old lover. Rushing down the stairs in flames, he had burned a pattern of footprints in the lilac stair carpet—all the way down from the second-story landing to the front door, and the varnished banister rails were blistered where he had run his blazing hands down them.

"Holy Christ," said Dudley Freeberg. "He must have gone through some kind of hell."

"Let's go upstairs," said Bonnie. She didn't want to think about any kind of hell, not today.

They went upstairs to the main bedroom and stared at the soaked, blackened, four-poster bed, with its burned velvet drapes. Behind the headboard hung a mirror that was cracked from one corner to the other and stained brown with smoke. Bonnie could see herself and Dudley Freeberg standing side by side like characters from an old sepia photograph.

Bonnie made notes. "The bed'll have to go, obviously, and the carpets, and I can erase the smoke damage. Like I said, you'll need the place repainted, but I can leave it like you wouldn't know that anything got burned here."

"Well, that sounds fine." Dudley Freeberg nodded. His face was waxy, and he was perspiring, and she could tell that he was close to suffering a panic attack. "Let's, uh, wrap this up outside, shall we?" He hurried downstairs, his feet zigzagging to avoid the burned patches on the carpet.

She sat in her car and wrote him an estimate while he stood with his coat over his arm and his necktie loosened, occasionally dabbing at his forehead with a crumpled-up Kleenex.

When she handed him the estimate, he almost snatched it from her. "Great. That looks good to me. I'll check with the family and then I'll call you."

"Any time," said Bonnie.

"Thanks for—" he said, nodding toward the house.

"Listen, this is something that nobody ever gets used to. You learn to deal with it, but you never get used to it. It's not something that a person *should* get used to."

"Well, thanks again."

He walked stiff-legged back to his car and drove off with a skittering squeal of tires. Bonnie watched him go, and then she walked back to her own car. As she did so, Kyle Lennox appeared, dressed in khaki chinos and a black polo shirt, and called out, "Hi, Bonnie! Before you go, Bonnie!"

She shaded her eyes with her hand. He came bounding across the street and said, "Hey, how was it?"

"Fine. Why?"

"Pretty grim in there, huh?"

"You wouldn't want to go in there unless you had to."

"Somebody told me the kid was—you know—actually"—he lowered his voice to a whisper—"*stuck to the door.*"

Bonnie shrugged. "I'm not really at liberty to discuss anything like that. I just clean up."

"He was stuck to the door, though, right?"

"Okay, yes. He was alight. He was trying to get out. He got stuck to the door."

Kyle Lennox shook his head slowly and admiringly and said, "That's such a gross-out. I don't know how you can do that stuff. I really don't."

"You act on TV. I don't know how you can do that, either. That would terrify me, acting on TV. I don't even like being in home videos."

"Listen," he said, "I'm having kind of a get-together tomorrow afternoon. You know, round-the-pool kind of thing. Just some friends from the studio and a couple of writers and one or two producers. Why don't you come along?"

"Excuse me?"

"I'm having a party, Bonnie, and I want you to come. I'd just love you to meet Gene Ballard. He's our director. He'll go crazy for you, I know it."

"I don't think I understand. What are you inviting me to a party for? You don't even know me."

"Hey! How well do you have to know anybody to like the way they look? How well do you have to know anybody to sincerely admire what they do? I really want you to come along, Bonnie. It's not going to be formal. You'll love it. All your favorite soap stars. And who knows? Gene may take a shine to you. He may even give you a walk-on part."

"When is it? This party?"

"Tomorrow evening, six o'clock, right here. Tell me you'll come."

Bonnie felt as if she were dreaming. This was really Kyle Lennox and he was really standing there and really inviting her to come to his show-business party round the pool.

"Yes," she said, and then she nodded. "Yes, okay. Why not?"

Bonnie Sees Her Mother

"Why didn't you tell me you were coming?" demanded her mother. "I could have made salad."

"Mom, it's okay. I don't want salad. I had a cheeseburger at Rusty's."

"Cheeseburger! Don't you know how much fat and salt they put in those things! No wonder you've put on so much weight."

"Oh, thanks. I think I've lost a couple of pounds as a matter of fact."

"You don't come for three weeks and now you come and you don't even tell me you're coming."

"Well, I'm here now. What are you complaining about?"

Mrs. Mulligan fussed around the living room, picking up *TV Guide*s and plumping cushions. She shooed her ginger tomcat, Marcus, off the couch because she knew that Bonnie didn't like it. The cat smelled rancid and had a terrible cackling hiss.

She was a short, full-figured woman, Mrs. Mulligan, with huge, white bouffant hair like a ball of cotton and tiny little hands and feet. She looked like Bonnie, if Bonnie were to blow out her cheeks and squeeze her eyes tightly shut. She lived in Reseda in a house that looked like every other house in Reseda: respectable, tidy, with a well-trimmed lawn and china ornaments on every available square inch of shelf. Bonnie's late father looked down from the living room wall with a strangely unbalanced grin that always reminded Bonnie of Alfred E. Neuman. It was a canvas-effect photograph in a gilded frame, with his fire department medals framed below.

Bonnie's five older brothers appeared in shoals of other framed photographs. Daryl when he graduated from the fire department academy. Robert when he got engaged to Nesta. Craig when he won the high school swimming trophy. Barry when he bought his first car. Richard when he broke his leg. Mark Hamill had signed the cast, and Mrs. Mulligan still had it in the garage.

The only picture of Bonnie was when she was twelve, at her first communion. Bonnie looked so sweet and innocent in her white silk dress that she could look at herself as a child now and she could almost cry for her. So trusting, so full of hope.

"The job I have to keep this place tidy," said her mother. "Richard leaving his socks everywhere."

"Mom, as usual, it's immaculate."

"You should have told me you were coming. I could have cleaned up."

"Why doesn't Richard put his own socks away?"

Her mother looked at her as if she were speaking a foreign language. Socks? Richard? His own? Away put?

In the kitchen, Bonnie said, "I feel like going to Hawaii." Her mother was arranging a plateful of butterscotch brownies and coconut squares. "Just me. By myself. I feel like packing a bag and going to Hawaii. I want to stand on a hill and watch a volcano erupting."

"A volcano? What about your family?"

"What about *me*?"

Her mother carried the tray of coffee and cookies into the living room. "You shouldn't have started that dreadful cleaning business. It's not healthy."

"It gives me satisfaction. It gives me the feeling that I'm making a difference."

"What difference? It's enough to make you feel ill."

"Isn't that a woman's role in life? Cleaning up? Look at you. You've spent your entire adult life cleaning up."

"Yes, but people's bodies. It doesn't bear thinking about."

"I don't clean up bodies, Mom. The coroner's department does that. Well, sometimes I clean up *bits* of bodies. Hair, teeth, stuff like that. I found seven toes the other day, underneath a tumble dryer. Guy killed his girlfriend with a chainsaw."

Her mother flapped her hand in disgust. "I don't want to think about it. If that Duke would get up off his backside and find himself a job, you wouldn't have to do it. By the way, how *is* Duke?"

"Pretty much the same. He went for an interview at the Century Plaza. Bar work."

"I could never understand what you saw in that man."

"I know you didn't. You never stopped telling me. Even now you don't stop telling me."

"What about your other job? The cosmetics thing?"

"I think I lost it. Maybe it was too . . . menstrual."

Bonnie's mother stared at her. "I'm sure I don't know what on God's good earth you're talking about sometimes, Bonnie Mulligan."

Bonnie carefully set down her coffee cup. "Mom . . . what would you do if a rich and famous TV personality invited you to a party?"

"What? What are you talking about now? *Party?*"

Bonnie had promised herself that she wouldn't tell anybody about Kyle Lennox because she desperately wanted to keep it a secret. She felt that, if she told her mother or Duke or Ray or any of her friends, it would turn out that she had misunderstood what Kyle Lennox said, or maybe the party would just turn out to be a big disappointment, with nobody famous there at all, and she would end up looking like a fool.

But she was so excited about it that she had to talk about it somehow, to somebody.

"A party. Like, you know, just some TV actors, and some TV producers, people like that. Not formal. Just a kind of a poolside thing. Champagne, maybe. Swimming."

"Who's going to invite me to anything like that?"

"A famous TV personality."

"I don't know any famous TV personalities."

"I know. But supposing you did. Supposing you knew—I don't know—Kyle Lennox?"

Her mother stared at her for a long time, steadily chewing a cookie with her false teeth. "I can't understand a word, Bonnie, I swear to God."

Bonnie looked up at the picture of her father with his cheesy smile. He had shot himself in the garage when Bonnie was fifteen and she could remember his blood being hosed down the driveway. And nobody had understood why.

RALPH RELENTS

That afternoon, around four o'clock, the hospital called and said that Ray could come home. Duke didn't want to miss *All My Children*, so Bonnie took the Buick and drove over to pick Ray up. The sky was a deep reddish color, as if God were using a strawberry filter. The temperature was dropping, too, and Bonnie felt that something strange was going to happen.

She found a space at the far end of the hospital parking lot, but before she could climb out of the car her cell phone played Henry Mancini's "Dear Heart." She flipped the phone open and said, "Bonnie's Trauma Scene Clean. How can we help you?"

"Bonnie, it's Ralph."

"Ralph! Hi, Ralph."

"I just called to make sure that your boy was okay."

"He's okay. I'm at the hospital now to pick him up."

"That's good. What about the assault charges?"

"I haven't heard yet. But I think there's a reasonable chance that the police won't pursue it. You know, first offense, good character, plus his mom's a personal friend of Captain O'Hagan."

"Well, I hope things work out okay."

"Okay. Thanks. How was Pasadena?"

"I—ah—wanted to apologize about that."

"You don't have to apologize. You needed me there and I couldn't go. That's all there is to it."

"As a matter of fact, I postponed it till Friday evening. It suited the buyers better. They had so many presentations to see yesterday that they were running nearly a day late."

"I see. Well, good luck."

"Ah—I was wondering if—well, I was wondering if you'd still like to come with me."

Bonnie climbed out of the car and slammed the door twice.

"I'm not fired?" she asked.

"That was me being irritable. Of course you're not fired. Do you think I'd fire one of my very favorite salespersons?"

"So I'm not fired and you want me to go to Pasadena with you Friday?"

"If you can get into the office by two-thirty?"

"I don't know, Ralph. What time are we supposed to get back?"

"There's kind of a business breakfast and then we

leave right away. Come on, tell me you'll come along."

"I'm not so sure, Ralph. Somebody has to take care of Ray. Cook him some supper and everything."

"Can't Duke do that?"

"Duke thinks eggs come out of chickens already fried."

"Can't they survive on takeout for just one night?"

"I don't know, Ralph. Ray's kind of messed up at the moment. I really don't like to leave him."

"Well, it's your choice. But I wish you'd change your mind."

"Let me think about it. I'll call you."

She switched off her cell phone and went up the hospital steps.

RETURN OF THE HERO

Ray's wrist and ankle were still in plaster, and he could only hop and hobble his way to the bathroom. Both of his eyes were spectacularly rainbow-colored, and his lips were still swollen. But the doctor had said that he was making excellent progress, and besides, they needed the bed. Ray was pleased because the hospital food was "drek."

Bonnie cooked pork and beans for supper, which was Ray's favorite, with Bisquick blueberry-lemon coffee cake for dessert. Duke drank three cans of Budweiser, and every time he lifted his can he said, "Here's to the hero. Here's to the goddamned hero."

After the seventh or eighth time, he began to get on Bonnie's nerves. "Oh, you think because he beat up on some totally innocent Mexican kids he's a hero?"

"He stood up for what's right, didn't he? And what's right, sweet cheeks, is that California belongs to Californians and not to the goddamned Mexicans. Do you know that this year there are going to be more goddamned Hispanics living in California than there are white people, and that's not counting the goddamned blacks?"

"Do you want some more of these fried potatoes?"

"Don't change the subject, Bonnie. The boy's a hero. In fact, he's not a boy anymore. He's a man. If I'd known he was going out to beat up on those goddamned wetbacks, I would've gone with him. *Then* they would have learned their lesson. Whop! Whap! Take that, you enchilada-eating ball of grease!"

"You're a bigot, Duke."

"A bigot? You're calling me a bigot? You're working your goddamned butt off all the hours that God sends you because some Mexican took my job and you think I'm a *bigot*? Under the circumstances I think I'm a model of goddamned tolerance. Under the circumstances I think I'm a goddamned *saint*."

Bonnie said, "There's still a chance that the police are going to file charges. I hope you're going to be saintly about that."

"If they charge him—well, that's the kind of price that heroes have to pay. But I'm behind you all the way, Ray. Your old man's behind you all the way. You've earned his respect, boy."

Ray gave Duke a split-lipped smile. Bonnie, spooning out potatoes, suddenly realized what Ray had done. In one stroke, he had ended all of the arguments between them by electing to side with his father, right or wrong. She supposed she couldn't blame him. Up until this evening, almost every mealtime had been World War Three, with Bonnie holding her ground against everything that Duke could throw at her, followed by Duke's noisy and abusive retreat. But now it was two against one, and there was nothing she could do but accept that what Duke said went, no matter how prejudiced or illogical it was.

Duke was right about one thing: Ray had gone down to the X-cat-ik Pool Bar as a boy and come back as a sort of a man.

After the meal, Bonnie helped Ray to heave his way back to his room and climb into bed.

Ray said, "You're not still mad at me, are you?"

"Mad at you? Why should I be mad at you? You're my only son."

"You shouldn't be mad at Dad, either."

"I'm not really mad at him. I just don't happen to look at life the same way that he does. He's full of expectations, but he never does anything to make them come true, and then he gets disappointed. But you can't go through your whole life being disappointed. Not if you won't make the effort."

"I love you, Mom. But, you know, Dad's my dad, too."

Bonnie nodded and gave him a pursed little smile, but it was then that she made up her mind that she would go to Pasadena, after all.

When she got back, Duke had opened another can of Budweiser and was sitting on the couch staring at *Stargate SG1*.

"Look at this shit. Can't they see what those aliens

are doing? Why don't they blow the shit out of them and have done with it?"

Bonnie sat down beside him and helped herself to a handful of caramel popcorn. "Ralph's asked me to go to Pasadena Friday."

There was a long silence while Duke swallowed beer. Then he burped and said, "Ralph? That asshole. I thought he fired you."

"He did, but now he wants me to take a trip to Pasadena."

Duke nonchalantly flung his arm around her and sniffed. "I hope you got great pleasure out of telling him to stick his trip to Pasadena where you don't need Ray-Bans."

"No, I'm going to say yes."

Duke slowly turned his head and stared at her. "You said *yes*? As in, 'Yes, I'm going to take a trip to Pasadena'?"

"Yes, I said yes."

"So how long are you supposed to be going for?"

"Just one night. Back on Saturday morning."

"You don't seriously think I'm going to let you spend a night in Pasadena with that creep?"

"Duke, he isn't a creep. He's my boss. And going to Pasadena is part of my job. He's not interested in my body. He's just interested in the fact that I'm good at presenting the product."

"Presenting the product? Oh, sure, I'll bet. Ralph Kosherick has only one thing on his mind, and that's getting you to present the product between your legs."

"Duke, don't be so crude. And don't be so ridiculous."

"Oh, I'm crude now, am I? Just because I don't want my wife to spend the night with some drooling what's-it's-name—lecher."

"Going to Pasadena is important, Duke. It's our major presentation for the holiday season. It could make all the difference between Glamorex really succeeding or going bankrupt."

"And I'm supposed to give a shit about that?"

"Duke, I need the Glamorex job, and more than that, I enjoy it. It fulfills me. For a few hours every day it makes me feel like a woman instead of a cleaner, or a housekeeper, or a taxi driver. I'm going to Pasadena whether you like it or not."

"I'm your fucking husband, for Christ's sake."

"Don't you be profane, Duke. I'm going."

"Didn't you hear me? I'm your husband."

"Husband? Who are you kidding? You're just some man who sits around my house all day and expects me to wash his clothes and cook his meals and work myself half to death to keep him in beer. Husband? You can't even get your dick up."

She wished instantly that she hadn't said that, of all things. She had always promised herself that she never would. She knew that you could say whatever you liked to a man—call him lazy and cruel and stupid and narrow-minded. But telling him that he couldn't get an erection was telling him that he wasn't a man at all. It opened up the floor right beneath his feet.

Duke didn't say a word. Instead, he lifted his can of Budweiser and poured beer slowly all over Bonnie's head. She sat on the couch with it dripping from her hair and running down the back of her neck.

"See what you fucking made me do?" said Duke. Then he leaned forward and screamed into her face at point-blank range, *"See what you fucking made me do?!"*

THE SECRET

She washed her hair and wrapped it in a pink towel turban. Earlier in the evening, for just a moment, she had been tempted to tell Duke about Kyle Lennox's invitation, but now she went to her purse and took out the business card with Kyle Lennox's autograph on it and tore it into the tiniest pieces possible.

TWO PHONE CALLS

A few minutes before 8:00 A.M. the next morning Bonnie received two phone calls. She was frying bacon for Duke's breakfast. The first call came from Lieutenant David Irizarry of the Los Angeles Police Department.

"Ms. Winter? Captain O'Hagan asked me to call you."

"Oh, yes?"

"It's about your son, Raymond Winter. Captain O'Hagan says that we've decided not to file charges of assault against him. However, he will be required at some point to come down to headquarters."

"I see. I see. That's good news, I guess."

"Captain O'Hagan will be in touch with you."

"Thank you. I appreciate it."

The second call was from Lieutenant Dan Munoz.

"Bonnie? I'm glad I caught you. I've fixed up a job for you at Ivanhoe Drive by the Silver Lake Reservoir. Kind of messy, the kid-in-a-box case. How about meeting me three o'clock tomorrow. We can sort it all out. Who loves you, baby?"

Bonnie hung up the phone and stared at the bacon gradually shriveling in the pan. Duke appeared, wearing a sweaty T-shirt and droopy boxer shorts. He hadn't shaved or showered, and he staggered around the kitchen as if he were still drunk, which he probably was. Eventually he dragged out a chair and sat down, tilting wildly to one side.

"You think I don't love you, don't you?" he announced.

"Duke—forget it. I'm not saying anything."

"But you think—because I can't always get it up— you think that I don't love you."

"Did I say that?"

"Shit—you didn't have to say it. I can see it in your eyes."

"Well, okay, let's be frank. It would be nice if you could sometimes get it up."

Duke didn't answer, but stared at the place mat as if it would miraculously reveal the answers to all of his problems. Bonnie took a plate out of the oven and scraped six slices of bacon onto it, as well as hash browns, grilled tomato, and two fried eggs. She set it down in front of Duke's nose and said, "There. Don't ever tell me that I don't love you. Ever."

Duke poked at his bacon with his fork. "You're trying to murder me, aren't you? All this goddamned cholesterol. Well, fuck you."

"Duke, if I wanted to kill you, I wouldn't wait for you to die of a heart attack, believe me. I don't have the patience."

He began to stab his breakfast even more furiously, as if he were trying to kill it. "Fuck you! You're trying to murder me—that's what you're doing! You're trying to clog up my arteries and murder me!"

Bonnie lowered her head and sat and listened to Duke's ranting and didn't say a word. What else could she say? After a while she stood up and took his plate away and scraped his entire breakfast into the garbage can under the sink—eggs, bacon, hash browns, toast, everything. Duke sat and watched her, gripping his fork so tightly that he bent it.

"I'm going out this evening," Bonnie announced.

"Out? Who says?"

"I say. I'm going to Ruth's place, and we're going to polish our nails and eat cake and talk about what bastards men can be."

"Oh, really. And who's going to look after Ray? Your son's practically a cripple, one day out of the hospital, and you're going *out*?"

"Yes, I'm going out. Because Ray has two parents, not just one, and you're the other one. So you can look after him. There's meat loaf in the icebox. All you have to do is warm it up in the microwave."

"Now you listen, Bonnie—" Duke began. But at that moment Ray appeared in the doorway, hobbling on his aluminum walking sticks. "Hi, Mom! How's everything going? That bacon sure smells good!"

"It's in the fucking trash if you want it," said Duke. He stood up, slammed his chair against the table and pushed his way out of the kitchen.

WHAT SHE WORE

It took Bonnie over two hours to get ready because she couldn't decide what to wear. What had Kyle Lennox meant by "informal"? His idea of "informal" might be a fugi silk suit by Anne Klein, with strappy Blahnik sandals. She tried on the red dress with the big pink flowers that she had bought to go to Ruth's son's bar mitzvah, but apart from the fact that she had put on weight since last summer, she thought it made her look like the victim of a frenzied stabbing.

She tried her fawn slacks, but there was a bleach mark on the right knee. Then she tried her jeans, but she didn't want to walk around with a Lands End label if everyone else was going to be wearing Armani.

Duke came to the half-open bedroom door and stared at her for a while, as if he couldn't understand why she was making such a fuss about dressing up if she was only going to Ruth's, but the look she gave him discouraged him from making any smart remarks. Eventually he said, "I'm going to take Ray to the market to buy some beer. So long as I have to baby-sit this evening, I think I'm entitled to a little refreshment, don't you?"

"There's fifteen dollars in the Popeye jar."

"I know. I took it already."

"Well, don't be too long, will you? I have to leave at five-thirty sharp."

"Yes, *sir!*" Duke gave her a sarcastic salute and left. She went back to her wardrobe, jingling her way through the wire hangers in mounting desperation. All her clothes suddenly looked so cheap. *Make a decision. Make a decision. You're going to be meeting people who buy their clothes on Rodeo Drive. They won't have seen this dress in Wal-Mart.*

In the end she decided on her navy-blue slacks and her cream satin blouse with the ruffles. The slacks were comfortable and even if the blouse's ruffles looked a little country-and-western, they concealed the size of her breasts. She laid them out on the bed.

Then she thought: *If it's going to be a poolside party, will they expect me to go for a swim?* She'd better take a swimsuit in case. She rummaged through the bottom drawer of her dressing table and eventually found her spotted turquoise swimsuit, the one with the little skirt, but when she tried it on, she looked far too bulgy. Next she tried the purple Lycra swimsuit with the high-cut legs and that was better, even if the top was so tight that it gave her four breasts.

By 5:05 she was ready, but Duke still wasn't back

with the car. She watched TV for a while, nervously perched on the arm of the couch, holding her brown plastic pocketbook ready in her hand. Then she got up and looked out of the window. At 5:27 he still hadn't returned, so she went and stood outside in the street. Old Mr. Lenz came past with his balding Pomeranian and said, "Hi there, Bonnie. Not working today?"

"No, Mr. Lenz. Not working today." *Like—do I look like I'm working, in my new navy slacks and my ruffled satin blouse?*

Half past five came and went, and there was still no sign of Duke. She wished to God that she had told him to take her cell phone with him. She went back inside and primped her hair for the seventh time. She was beginning to feel hot and edgy now. Supposing Duke didn't come back at all? That meant that she would have to take her truck.

At 5:45 she wrote a note saying, "Gone To Ruth's Thanks For Nothing" and stuck it on the front of the icebox with a magnet in the shape of a heart.

PARTY PARTY

She parked the truck around the corner on Alta Avenue and walked the rest of the way. The street in front of Kyle Lennox's house was a traffic jam of shiny, expensive automobiles—a yellow Ferrari Testarossa, a silver Lamborghini and more Mercedes than Bonnie had ever seen in one street together at the same time.

Even out on the street she could hear the samba band playing "Samba em Preludio" with lazy, torpid, self-satisfied rhythm. Two pimply teenage car jockeys were standing on the lawn outside, wearing white coats with gold epaulets. They stared at Bonnie as she came walking up the street and up the red-brick pathway.

"Help you?" one of them asked her, showing his shiny wire braces.

"I've been invited to the party," said Bonnie.

The car jockey peered over her shoulder in bewilderment. "Where's your car, ma'am?"

"I didn't come by car."

"You *walked* here?"

"No, I was dropped at the corner by an alien spacecraft. Is this the right way in?"

"Sure. I have to check your invitation."

"I wasn't given an invitation."

"You were invited but you weren't given an invitation?"

At that moment, however, Kyle Lennox appeared on the porch, wearing a green silk shirt and flappy white pants and carrying a highball. He lifted his drink in salute and said, "Bonnie! Come along in! Real glad you could make it!"

Bonnie gave the car jockeys a "so-there" grimace and followed Kyle Lennox in through the front door. The stairs and the hallway were crowded with people, all of them shouting and shrieking so that they sounded like the passengers on a rapidly sinking liner. She felt a panicky urge to make her apologies and leave, but Kyle Lennox put his suntanned arm around her and propelled her through the throng until they reached the living room. And what a living room it was. She had never seen anything like it. The far wall was mirrored, floor to ceiling, and lined with bronze statuettes of naked nymphs. A huge crystal chandelier hung over the center of the room, and the chairs and the couches were all upholstered in cream-and-yellow satin. The patio windows were open to the pool area, which was paved in swirly Italian marble and equally crowded with laughing, screaming people. Beyond the pool, the garden was brilliant with scented flowers, and a white stone statue of Pan danced on a pedestal, his hair lifted into little horns.

"You probably know some of the people here already," Kyle Lennox shouted in her ear. The salsa band had launched into a Latin interpretation of "Positively Fourth Street," and a man in a red sombrero and tight red satin flares was weakly singing the words into a microphone. "There's Vanessa McFarlane from *Shining Light*, and Gus Hanson from *The Lives We Lead.*"

"Gus Hanson? Where? I can't believe it! It is. You're right. It's *Gus Hanson!*"

"You want to meet him? He's an old surfing buddy of mine."

"I don't know, I don't know. Let me catch my breath. I'm a little overwhelmed, to tell you the truth."

"Come and meet him. He's the nicest guy on the planet. But how about a drink first? We have champagne and wild white strawberries. You'll love it."

He waved to one of the waiters, who brought over a tray that was jingling with tall, trumpet-shaped champagne flutes. In each glass danced six or seven tiny wild strawberries, and the rims were sparkling with sugar.

"Hey . . . doesn't this look gorgeous?" said Bonnie. "I never thought of putting strawberries in champagne. Not that me and Duke can stretch to champagne very often. Well, when I say very often, I mean ever. Duke dropped a pickle in his beer once, but that was more by way of an accident."

Kyle Lennox steered Bonnie outside, to a white

cast-iron seat by the pool, where Gus Hanson was talking to six or seven giggly young girls with shining blond hair and long, suntanned legs. Gus Hanson had curly dark hair, a Roman nose, and a white silk shirt that was open to his navel. He wore thong sandals and no socks.

"Gus . . . this is the lady I was telling you about, the one who's going to be cleaning up the Marrin house."

Gus Hanson took off his gold-lensed sunglasses and grinned up at her. "Hi . . . great you could come. Kyle just won't stop talking about you. He says he can't believe that you do what you do."

"Well," said Bonnie, uncomfortably, "somebody has to do it. It's a service."

"You never think about it, though. You never think what happens after somebody goes crazy and kills their whole family. You never think that somebody has to mop it up."

"Is that what you *do*?" asked one of the long-legged blond girls, wrinkling up her tiny retroussé nose.

"Sure, that's what I do. I clean up after any kind of trauma. Like I say, it's a service."

"You've been in the Marrin house?" asked Gus Hanson.

"Of course. I have to give an estimate."

"I mean, what's it like in there? The room where they died?"

"It's burned, that's all. There's not much to see."

"The kid was stuck to the door," put in Kyle Lennox. "Can you imagine that? He was burning like a fucking torch, and he was trying to get out of the door, but he, like, melted to the paintwork."

"Holy shit," said Gus. "Can you actually *see* that in there? Like where he was stuck to the door?"

Bonnie was feeling hot and overdressed. She could feel perspiration sliding down her back into her waistband. She took a sip of champagne, but all the sugar stuck to her upper lip and gave her a white mustache. Kyle Lennox said, "Here," and used a linen napkin to brush it off, a gesture that was both intimate and deeply embarrassing. It made her feel like a child.

At that moment, a short, portly man came around the pool, his bald head shining like a dented brass doorknob, his eyes hidden behind black, thick-framed sunglasses. He was wearing a multicolored striped shirt, all reds and greens and yellows, and a loose pair of green linen pants. "Bonnie," said Kyle Lennox. "This is my producer, Gene Ballard. Gene, this is Bonnie."

Gene Ballard held out a chubby little hand, more like a pig's trotter than a hand, thick with lumpy gold rings. He smelled overpoweringly of Fahrenheit aftershave. "It's an amazing pleasure to meet you, my dear. Kyle has a talent for collecting all the most interesting people. You know who came to his last little get-together? Tasha Malova, that transvestite who got himself involved with the police commissioner. You should have seen him. Her. *It*, whatever. Beautiful, and I mean drop-dead stunning. But six-foot-three with a voice like a fucking foghorn, and a blue miniskirt right up to its ass." He gave a thick, phlegmy bellow of laughter and turned around to everybody standing by the pool to make sure that they were laughing, too.

Gus Hanson said, "Hey, Bonnie, is there anything you've ever refused to do, because it was so totally disgusting?"

"How about you?" Bonnie retorted. "Is there anything that *you've* ever refused to do?"

"Well, sure. I refused to pose for *Playgirl*."

"You refused to pose for *Playgirl*?"

"Absolutely." Gus Hanson pouted. "I want my image to be more about my work than the sex appeal or whatever. I mean, if it's a sex scene, of course I'm not going to have my shirt and tie on. But it's the whole point of focusing on the talent rather than the *fromage*."

"So," said Gene Ballard, taking hold of Bonnie by the elbow, "how does a pretty lady like you get into work like cleaning up corpses?"

"Oh, I don't clean up the remains. We call them remains. The coroner's department cleans up the remains. I just clean the trauma scene after the remains are removed. Curtains, carpets, stuff like that. It's just like being a regular cleaner, only obviously it's more specialized."

He nodded at her. She wished his sunglasses weren't quite so black. It was as if he didn't have any eyes.

"How long does it take you to film one episode of *The Wild and the Wayward*?" she asked him. "I mean, do you have to do lots of takes, or do you run through it all in one go?"

"But you *have* seen corpses?"

"Yes, well, of course I've seen corpses. But I don't get to see too many."

"What's the most gruesome one you ever saw?"

Bonnie was aware now that everybody was watching her, everybody was listening to her. The samba band had suddenly finished playing "Positively Fourth Street," with a chung-chung-chung flourish of guitars, and now there was only the laughing and the shouting from inside the house.

"I, uh, it's difficult for me to say. Everybody's passing is a tragedy."

Gene Ballard put his arm around Bonnie's waist and began rhythmically but discreetly to squeeze the spare tire that bulged above her waistband.

"You, um, ever see anybody with their head missing, anything like that?"

"I've seen a woman with her head missing, yes. That was in Culver City, about a year ago."

"How did it happen? I mean, how did she lose her head?"

"Her husband attacked her with a machete. He just went on chopping and chopping till he chopped her head clear off."

There was a horrified titter from one of the girls. Gene Ballard said, "When you saw her, this woman, where was she?"

"In the bedroom. A lot of these things happen in the bedroom. Late at night, you know, people get tired and drunk, or maybe they're stoned."

"A lot of blood, I'll bet?"

"Oh, yes." Bonnie tried to move herself away from his rhythmically squeezing fingers, but she couldn't.

Gus, on the cast-iron seat, casually propped his foot on the table in front of him and leaned back grinning. Kyle Lennox looked around at all of his friends as if to say, *What did I tell you? Is this a character, or what?*

"When you saw this woman, what? Was she wearing anything, or was she naked?"

"She was"—dry cough—"she was in the nude."

"So she was lying on the bed naked with no head? Lying on her back?"

"Listen, I don't really like to go into the details."

"Were her legs open, or were they closed?"

Bonnie reached behind her and firmly pushed his arm away. "Like I say, Mr. Ballard, every passing is a tragedy, and it's very personal to the people involved. I don't do this work because I'm some kind of voyeur."

"Hey, don't take offense! I'm not suggesting you're any kind of voyeur. I'm just interested to know what your work is all about. Come on, all of us here, we only deal in fiction, in stories. The only blood *we* ever get to see comes from special effects. But what you deal in, that's real life."

"So I've been told."

"So that was the worst you ever saw? The woman with a body but no head? Didn't you ever see a woman with a head but no body?"

Gus Hanson shouted with laughter. Kyle Lennox clapped. Bonnie said, "You're going to have to excuse me," and put her champagne glass down on the table. Gus swung his foot around too quickly and knocked it over so that it smashed on the marble flooring, and the wild strawberries rolled away.

"I'm sorry," Bonnie flustered. "That was an accident, really. Tell me how much it cost, and I'll buy you a new one."

Kyle Lennox smiled and shook his head. "It's Waterford crystal and it probably cost over a hundred and fifty dollars, but—come on, Bonnie, forget it."

Bonnie said, "I'm sorry," again and pushed her way back through the living room. One or two of the shrieking throng glanced at her in momentary curiosity, but then she was back out through the front door and on the street again. The two pimply car jockeys said, "Hey, going already?"

"I made a mistake," said Bonnie. She was trying to stop her voice from shaking. "Wrong party." She started to walk back along Lincoln Boulevard, the heels of her sandals clacking on the sidewalk.

"Bonnie!" called out Kyle Lennox. "Bonnie, come back here!"

She didn't turn around. She just wanted to keep on walking until she reached her truck and never think about Kyle Lennox or *The Wild and the Wayward* ever again. She cursed herself for her vanity. Why did she think that Kyle Lennox had invited her? Because she was beautiful, or wealthy, or famous, or smart? How could she have walked into a TV star's party wearing a ruffled blouse that made her look like a waitress in a roadside diner and a pair of pants with all of her fat bulging over? And a vinyl handbag, with a purple Lycra swimsuit in it?

Kyle Lennox ran a little way after her, but then he gave a dismissive wave of his hand and turned back to his get-together. Bonnie turned the corner just as a traffic cop was tucking a parking ticket under the windshield of her truck.

In the Dark That Night

Bonnie's eyes welled with scalding-hot tears, and she curled herself up tightly, as tight as she could, in an effort to comfort herself. She didn't want to cry, but the pain in her throat was too great, and she couldn't stop herself from letting out a rasping honk of misery.

She let out another honk, and then another, and then she started to sob so bitterly that she could hardly breathe.

Duke sat up in bed. "What the fuck are you laughing at?"

She tried to catch her breath, but she couldn't.

"It's two-thirty in the morning. What's so fucking funny?"

"I'm not laughing," she said, wiping her face on the sheet. "I'm crying."

"You're crying?" There was a long, exasperated silence. "What are you crying for?"

"I don't know, Duke. I guess I must have had a sad dream."

"You had a sad dream? You had a sad dream so you have to make a noise like a whale?"

"I'm sorry."

"Yeah, well do me a favor and go back to sleep. And for God's sake, don't have any dreams about being happy."

Bonnie wiped her eyes with her fingers and sniffed. "No, Duke. I won't do that."

Pasadena, Where the Grass Is Greener

"Phil, this is Bonnie. Bonnie, this is Phil Cafagna, head of purchasing for Pacific Pharmacy."

A silvery-haired man in a silvery three-piece suit kissed Bonnie's hand and said, "Charmed. I always said that Ralph had exceptional taste."

"Bonnie's been doing some really excellent work for us, Phil. Helped to boost our turnover by over six percent this year."

"Well, I can see why." Phil smiled. He was deeply tanned, with glittery blue eyes, and he vaguely reminded Bonnie of Blake Carrington in *Dynasty*. His hair appeared to be ruffled up into two demonic horns, and on closer inspection Bonnie realized that it was a hairpiece.

"I'll catch you later, Bonnie." Phil winked at her and walked away across the hotel lobby.

Ralph said, sotto voce, "You need to watch yourself with that guy. He gives wolves a bad name."

"He's not much of an advertisement for toupees, either."

Ralph pressed his finger to his lips. "If Phil Cafagna likes what he sees, he can turn our whole business around. Pacific Pharmacy has two-hundred-eighty outlets, under different names, all the way from Eureka to San Diego."

"So long as that doesn't mean I have to run my hands through his rug."

Bonnie and Ralph were standing in line in the blue-carpeted lobby of the Ramada Inn on East Colorado Boulevard, in Pasadena. The lobby was already crowded with buyers and salespeople from dozens of different stores and pharmacies, and there was an overwhelming smell of heavy-duty perfume. Bonnie was wearing her pink waxed-cotton suit, but compared with the rest of the cosmetics representatives, she felt distinctly underdressed and under made-up. Ralph had bought himself a natty new sports coat and fastened an orchid in his lapel, but the cuffs of his pants were still swinging an inch above his Gucci loafers.

"Okay, here's how it goes. Our main presentation is at seven . . . then there's cocktails and general mingling, with six separate demonstrations and a special Moist-Your-Eyes promotion. We can run through it as soon as we've checked in."

"Ralph . . . I want to thank you for giving me another chance."

"Don't be stupid. I shouldn't have fired you in the first place. You have a family, after all."

"Well, it's kind of a family."

"Still having problems with Duke?"

"How do you know about that?"

"We work in a small company, Bonnie. There isn't much I don't know. Especially when it affects somebody I really care about."

"Yes, well. Things will work themselves out."

The Glamorex evening went even better than Bonnie had expected. All of the products had been filmed at well-known soap-opera locations, and each had a passionate, panting soap opera–style script that told a woman how she could use My Mystery eye shadow to make herself look like a millionairess or Angel Glitter body lotion to win over the hunk of her dreams. Young girls in glittering sequin minidresses performed a funky dance routine at the Insomnia coffee house from *The Bold and the Beautiful* to show off the new range of Disco Nights nail polish. Two sophisticated couples dined at The Colonnade Room from *The Young and the Restless* to promote Loving Embrace hairspray.

After the video presentation, waiters brought round sparkling wine and canapés. Two professional beauticians, twin sisters, demonstrated all of Glamorex's new lines. Ralph privately called them The Lobotomized Barbies. Phil Cafagna came up to Bonnie after she had given her spiel about Moist-Your-Eyes and raised his glass to her.

"You're quite a commercial asset, Bonnie. Ralph's a lucky man."

"He's a good boss, Mr. Cafagna."

"Oh, call me Phil, for Christ's sake. How about a glass of wine?"

He lifted a glass from a passing tray and handed it to her. "Let's drink to something," he said. "Here's to the real face that hides behind the painted mask."

Bonnie wasn't sure what he meant, but she clinked glasses with him anyhow.

"How about you, Bonnie?" he asked. "What's your face really like, when you're not selling Glamorex cosmetics? What kinda person are you?"

"I'm a wife and a mother."

"I didn't mean that. Being a wife and a mother defines your relationship with other people. That doesn't tell me what kind of a person you are."

"I'm not so sure that I know what kind of person I am. A good one, I hope. Somebody who looks after other people when they need me the most."

"I'm sure you do. You strike me as a deeply caring woman. But you also strike me as a woman who's never had the opportunity to break free and be herself."

Bonnie gave him a little shake of her head to indicate that she didn't really understand what he was talking about.

He took hold of her arm and walked her toward the French windows. Outside the night was breezy and warm, and Bonnie could hear music playing from the ballroom.

"I work with women all day, every day, and I think I know something about them," said Phil. "These days, they have their careers and they have their independence and they can do pretty much anything they like. But do you know something? They're still trapped. Everybody's trapped, until they can find somebody to set them free. That's what you need, Bonnie. You need somebody to give you the key and let you out."

They strolled along the covered cloisters, with the overhanging creeper rustling softly. The band was playing a syrupy version of Lyle Lovett's song "Nobody Knows Me," and for the first time in years, Bonnie felt peaceful and relaxed and even romantic.

"How about another glass of wine?" Phil suggested.

"I don't think so. We have an early breakfast tomorrow. Then we have to be getting back to L.A."

Phil stopped and looked her straight in the eye. "You're a great-looking woman, Bonnie. You've got everything going for you. It really disturbs me to see a woman like you in so much pain."

"I'm not in pain, Phil. I'm an ordinary workingwoman like every other ordinary workingwoman."

"You think so? I know pain. I can feel pain a mile off."

Bonnie shrugged. "I can't say that I don't have problems."

"Your husband never sees you for what you are."

"To be frank with you, Phil, I don't think he sees me at all."

"Your kids give you nothing but trouble."

"Kid. We only have one—Ray, he's fifteen. But what can you expect? All kids are trouble when they're growing up."

"So what are you going to do?"

"Do? What do you expect me to do? I'm going to go home tomorrow just like always."

"Supposing I said don't."

"I have to go home, Phil. What else would I do?"

"You could spend the rest of the week with me. We could go sailing off Catalina Island. We could walk on the seashore and eat lobster dinners and drink champagne."

Bonnie smiled and shook her head.

"I'll tell you something, Bonnie," said Phil. "A lot of people think that I'm some kind of Casanova, picking up women and taking them to bed and then going on to the next. But the fact of the matter is that I can't stand to see women who never get the chance to be themselves. Their husbands don't allow them to break free because they'll be too demanding; and their employers don't allow them to break free because they might ask for what they really deserve. So on they go, year after year, until one day they realize that practically their whole life has passed them by, and they've lost their looks, and all they've got to look forward to is old age. That's a prison sentence, in my book.

"I get my kicks out of letting women out on parole. I get my kicks out of showing them what exciting and interesting and attractive people they really are. Sometimes there's sex and sometimes there isn't. That's not important. What's important is the sheer joy of flinging the cell door open and saying, 'Come on, come out and play for a while. No strings, no responsibilities, no recriminations. Just let yourself dance around in the open air.'"

Bonnie finished the last of her sparkling wine. Then she stood on tiptoe and gave Phil a kiss on each cheek. "Can I say something?" she said.

"Sure. You're a free agent. You may not believe it, but you can say whatever you want."

"No strings, no responsibilities, no recriminations?"

"Not a one."

"What you said to me just then . . . about letting me out on parole . . . that's the most patronizing bullshit I ever heard in my entire life."

She was smiling so sweetly that—for three full seconds—he didn't realize what she had said to him. Then, gradually, his face went through a complicated series of changes, as if it were searching for an expression that would allow him to continue talking to her with as much dignity as possible.

"You think that's patronizing bullshit?" he said, at last. His voice was controlled, but there was an unmistakable edge in it.

"In my opinion, yes. Speaking as somebody who works with men all day, every day."

"In that case, I guess you and I won't be spending the night together, then?"

"I think that's highly unlikely."

"I see. Just like it's highly unlikely that Pacific Pharmacy is going to place a single order for Glamorex cosmetics?"

"What is that, a threat?"

"No, darling. You should know. It's just patronizing bullshit."

She found Ralph in the bar, happily knocking back whiskey sours. She sat down next to him and asked the barman for a white wine spritzer. Actually she felt like a beer, but she was thinking about her figure.

"Let's celebrate," said Ralph, raising his glass. "We've taken more orders tonight than we've taken in the past six months. And I give you most of the credit."

"Ralph—"

"Don't be modest. You were terrific. You had Phil Cafagna eating out of your hand. I can't even believe that I thought about firing you. You'll forgive me, won't you?"

"Ralph, there's nothing to forgive."

"Oh, but there is. The truth is, Bonnie, I was jealous. I wanted to take you to Pasadena, but then you couldn't go because you had a husband and a son. And I admit it: I was jealous."

"Ralph, you don't have anything to be jealous about."

"Yes, I do." He leaned forward and focused his eyes on her as if he were trying to make absolutely sure that he was talking to the right person. "I'm in love with you, Bonnie. That's the point. I've been in love you ever since I first saw you, except that I love you twice as much now as I did then, if that makes any sense."

"Ralph, you've had too many whiskey sours."

"Of course I have. But they've given me the courage to tell you how I really feel, that's all. You're the most desirable woman I've ever met."

"I'm very flattered, Ralph, but you're a married man and I'm a married woman."

"What difference does that make? You know and I know that we're both married to the wrong people."

"Ralph, there's something I have to tell you. Something very serious."

"Ssh, don't say anything. Don't spoil the illusion."

"What illusion?"

"The illusion that people might have that you and I are sitting here as a couple, and that when we've finished these drinks we're going to take a bottle of champagne upstairs and go to bed together."

"That's some illusion."

Ralph took off his glasses. "Is it?" he asked her.

ON RALPH'S NIGHTSTAND

Bonnie opened her eyes. On the nightstand next to her were:

Ralph's eyeglasses
Ralph's stainless-steel Sekonda wristwatch
One Glamorex promotional ballpoint pen
One half-finished roll of Tums
Eighty-six cents in change
One Ramada notepad with the word "Ecstasy"
  scrawled on it

THE NEXT MORNING

The next morning Ralph made love to her again, in silence. He moved up and down on her very slowly, like a man taking a relaxing swim, and all the time he never took his eyes off her once.

Without his glasses he looked years younger, and almost handsome. His body, too, was surprisingly muscular and athletic. He breathed steadily through his nose, and every now and then he dipped his head down to kiss her.

When he climaxed, he gripped the hair at the back of her neck and pressed her face close to his chest. He made her feel as if he wanted to bury her inside of himself, so that he could keep her and protect her for ever.

Afterward, they lay side by side with the morning sun falling across the bed in bright geometric bars.

"Well—I guess we'd better be getting up soon,"

said Ralph, picking up his watch and peering at it shortsightedly. "The promotional breakfast starts at eight."

Bonnie drew a circle on his shoulder with her finger. "It's funny, isn't it? Duke was convinced that you were going to get me into bed, but I told him you didn't have a snowball's chance in hell."

"You're not sorry?"

"I'm only sorry that I didn't do this years ago. I'd forgotten what it was like. How good it can be."

Ralph said, "It's not just the sex. It's the personality. Vanessa has about as much personality as an empty suitcase."

"You're a good lover, Ralph."

He kissed her. "I don't want this to end here, Bonnie."

"We both have responsibilities, Ralph. We're not carefree kids anymore."

"I still don't want this to end here."

She sat up. She didn't know what to say to him because she didn't understand what had happened to her. She felt excited, yes, and flattered, and daring. But the world into which she had woken up this morning was a very different place from the world she had lived in yesterday. Everything looked the same, but everything had changed around, as if scene shifters had been at work while she slept.

She climbed out of bed and went naked to the window with one hand held self-consciously over her stomach. Ralph stayed where he was and watched her as she opened the drapes. "I feel like running away," she said. She turned and smiled at him. "I feel like running away and never going back."

"We can, if you want to."

"No, we can't. We both have businesses to run, people who count on us."

"We can sell up, and move to the Bay Area, and be hippies for the rest of our lives."

"Nice dream, Mr. Kosherick."

"It doesn't have to be a dream, Mrs. Winter."

She came and sat on the edge of the bed and ran her fingers lightly through his hair. "You've done me a whole lot of good—did you know that?"

"I know. You've done the same for me. That's why I don't want it to end."

"Well, we'll see," she said, kissing him on the forehead.

THE KID-IN-A-BOX CASE

She parked her truck close up behind Dan Munoz's Chevrolet, climbed down from the cab and walked across the hot concrete driveway. Dan was waiting by the front door, talking to a wizened, seventyish man in a beige safari suit.

"Hi, Bonnie."

"Hi, Dan. Nice necktie."

"Thanks, it's Armani. Bonnie—this is the landlord, George Keighley. He's going to show you around the place so that you can give him a price. George, this is Bonnie Winter, the best cleanup lady in town. In fact she's the cleanup queen."

George Keighley gave a racking cough and acknowledged Bonnie with a nod. His skin was the color of oxidized liverwurst, and he had huge, hairy ears, like those of a Hobbit.

The house on Ivanhoe Drive was painted bright yellow with bright green shutters and a bright red roof, so that it looked as if its color scheme had been chosen by a six-year-old child. George Keighley led the way into the small entrance hall, which was stuffy and airless and inexplicably cluttered with five dining room chairs. Then they went through to the living area, an awkward L-shaped room that was furnished with ill-matched couches and armchairs and a 1960s coffee table with orange wooden balls for feet.

"Did you see this case on TV?" asked Dan.

"No, I didn't. What happened?"

"The house was rented by a twenty-four-year-old guy called David Hinsey and his girlfriend, Maria Carranza, who was twenty-two. Hinsey worked for a TV repair company, and Carranza worked on the checkout at Kwik-Mart. They had a two-and-a-half-year-old son, Dylan. The trouble was, they couldn't afford a baby-sitter, so before she went to work Carranza used to shut Dylan in a large cardboard grocery box and seal it with duct tape so that he couldn't get out. She punched the box full of air holes, and she gave the kid a mug of orange juice and a pack of Oreos to eat. She left the television on, too, so that he could watch it through a little slit."

"Oh, God," said Bonnie. "How long was he left like that?"

"Six or seven hours at a stretch. Sometimes longer if Hinsey worked overtime. The neighbors didn't even realize that he and Carranza *had* a kid."

George Keighley said, "In here," and coughed some more. He led the way past a musty-smelling bathroom with a pale green bath and a shower with a crack in the door, until they reached the main bedroom. "I've had to keep the windows closed in case of vandals, so it stinks some."

He opened the door and Bonnie immediately smelled the rotting-chicken stench of decomposing blood. She stepped inside and looked around. The cheap orange drapes were all drawn so that it took a moment for her eyes to grow accustomed to the gloom. All the same, she felt at once that appalling atmosphere that characterized every trauma scene she ever walked into—the feeling that something unthinkable had happened here—a scenario straight from hell.

On one side of the room were two single beds, pushed close together. They had no bedding on them except for two worn-out mattresses with blue-ticking covers. Both mattresses were heavily stained with dark brown blood, and on the magnolia-colored wall behind them was a wild array of handprints and semicircular smears of dried blood and excrement.

Dan said, "The reason that Hinsey and Carranza couldn't afford a baby-sitter was because they spent all of their earnings on speed and crack cocaine. Nobody will ever know what happened for sure, but it looks like Hinsey came home and found that Carranza had helped herself to his stash while he was at work. There was obviously an argument, a struggle, and Hinsey stabbed Carranza with a kitchen knife. Not just once, which would have been enough to kill her, but two hundred and seven times. All over. Even her face."

"Then what?" asked Bonnie. She hunkered down on the pale green carpet so that she could examine a brown rectangular stain.

"Then Hinsey must have realized what he'd done and killed himself. Committed *seppuku*, as a matter of fact. Stabbed himself in the stomach, first this way, then that way, crisscross, so that his intestines fell out on the bed. The M.E. said it probably took him over three hours to die."

"Messy," said Bonnie.

Dan stood beside her as she raked her fingers through the stained carpet pile to see how deep it was and what it was made of. High polyester content, fortunately.

"Of course the kid was left in the cardboard box and couldn't get out. He was in there for nearly a week before he died of dehydration. He was so hungry that he even ate pieces of cardboard."

Bonnie stood up, too. "This was where the box was standing?" she asked, pointing down at the rectangular stain.

"That's right. Nobody at the TV repair company bothered to find out why Hinsey hadn't been into work because he was always so unreliable anyway. The same with Carranza. In the end Mr. Keighley came around for the monthly rent, and that was when they were found. The M.E. estimates that they were lying here dead for well over three weeks. The kid was swollen so much that he burst the box."

Bonnie took a last look around the room. "This shouldn't set you back too much, Mr. Keighley. I can dispose of the mattresses and clean the walls and the carpet for you. I can spray for coffin-fly infestation, too. Let's say a round six hundred."

"Six hundred? Jesus Christ. No wonder they call you the cleanup queen."

"That's the price, Mr. Keighley. You won't find anybody else to touch it for less. In fact, you probably won't be able to find anybody else to touch it at all."

"You're getting the very best here, sir," said Dan, laying his hand on Bonnie's shoulder.

Mr. Keighley blew out his cheeks. "Okay, then, if that's what it takes. How soon can you do it?"

They watched George Keighley drive away in his elderly but highly polished black Cadillac.

"You know who that car used to belong to?" said Dan. "Neil Reagan—Ronnie's older brother."

"Ronald Reagan had an *older* brother?"

"Sure. Hard to believe, isn't it?" Dan took out one of his bright green cigars. "Is there something different about you today?" he asked her.

"I don't know. What do you mean?"

"You look different. I can't put my finger on it. Maybe it's your hair."

Bonnie shrugged. But she knew what he was talking about. After her night in Pasadena, she definitely *felt* different. Intoxicated, almost.

She said, "There was something I wanted to talk to you about. I found some chrysalis kind of things at the Glass residence and some caterpillars at the Goodman apartment. I took one of the caterpillars up to Howard Jacobson at UCLA just to see what it was. He said it was a butterfly, but quite a rare kind of butterfly."

"And?"

"Well, I don't know, really. But he said this particular butterfly has a bad reputation in Mexican folklore. It's the daytime disguise of some evil goddess. She's supposed to drive people crazy so that they kill the people they love the most."

Dan lit his cigar and puffed out smoke. "So what are you telling me? Aaron Goodman was possessed? He ran a dry-cleaning business. Dry cleaners don't get possessed."

"No, of course not. But Howard said that you never find this butterfly outside of a certain part of Mexico. And there's kind of a Mexican connection, isn't there? There was a Mexican sugar skull at the Glass residence, wasn't there? And there was a painting of Mexican guys in hats at the Marrin house. And the Goodmans had a Mexican maid."

"Oh, sure. The Goodmans and a million-and-a-half other families in Los Angeles."

"I'm not saying any of this *means* anything, but I thought you might be interested, that's all."

Dan said, "I'd rather leave the bugs and the maggots to you, sweet cheeks. Are you sure I can't buy you dinner?"

DUKE'S FAVORITE

That evening she made Duke's favorite supper:

2½ lbs pork ribs
2 cups pineapple juice
3 tablespoons soy sauce
3 tablespoons sesame oil
4 cloves chopped garlic
Hot red-pepper flakes
2 teaspoons chopped ginger root

She simmered the ribs in pineapple juice until almost all of it had evaporated, then tossed them in the rest of the ingredients so that they could marinate for thirty minutes. Then she baked them in a hot oven until they were crispy.

"To what do I owe this pleasure to?" asked Duke, with marinade glistening on his chin.

"I don't know. I just thought it was time we started trying to be nice to each other."

Duke sniffed and wiped his mouth with the back of his hand.

"You look different. You wearing some kind of different eye shadow or something?"

"Unh-hunh. Same old Midnight Caress."

"Who thinks these stupid things up, huh? Midnight Caress."

Bonnie helped herself to salad, and thought of Ralph's hand reaching across the bed in the small hours of the morning and gently cupping her breast.

"Any beans left?" asked Ray.

"Sure." Bonnie stood up. "You want some more, Duke?"

CLEANING UP AGAIN

Monday morning they started by dragging down the orange drapes. They opened the windows wide, too, to get rid of the smell of blood. Between them, wearing their bright yellow protective suits, Bonnie and Esmeralda carried the two single mattresses out to the truck, and Bonnie pulled one of the drapes over them.

When they shifted the beds away from the wall, they found that something rancid and indescribable had slid down the wall onto the skirting board, and the corner of the room was thick with maggots. Esmeralda brought in the vacuum cleaner and sucked them all up. They made a soft pattering sound inside the vacuum cleaner's hose, almost like rain falling on a dry day.

"How was Pasadena?" asked Esmeralda.

"Okay. It was okay."

Bonnie got down on her hands and knees and sprayed stain remover on the rectangular brown mark on the carpet. As she scrubbed, she tried not to think about what she was actually cleaning up, but the horror of it suddenly and unexpectedly overwhelmed her, like a huge, cold wave. She stood up— she had to stand up—and when she did so, she almost fainted.

"Bonnie? What's the matter?"

"Dan Munoz said—"

"Dan Munoz said what?"

"Dan Munoz said he tried to eat cardboard."

"Who? What are you talking about?"

"The kid in the box. He was starving to death, so he tried to eat cardboard."

"Hey, you're looking terrible. Why don't you go sit in the truck for a while?"

"I—no, I'll be okay."

"No, you won't. You're white like a sheet. I can finish the vacuuming."

Bonnie took two or three deep breaths, but she lost her balance and nearly fell over, and she was sweating the way she always did when her period was due.

"Just give me a couple of minutes. I didn't eat breakfast—that's the trouble."

"You want me to help you?"

"I'm fine, I'm fine. You just carry on."

She went outside. It was hot, but there was a slight breeze blowing from the southwest, and it cooled the sweat on her forehead. She climbed up into the cab of her truck, opened the 7-Up cooler in which she always brought her breakfast and took out a chilled bottle of Diet Coke. She swallowed some, but it rushed straight back up again and it ran out of her nose.

She had never felt as bad as this before, even when she had cleaned up a crib in which twin baby sisters had been lying for over two months. Her hands were shaking, and when she looked at herself in the rear-view mirror she saw that her lips looked completely bloodless. "Take it easy," she told herself. "Count to ten and think about nothing at all."

After five minutes, she began to feel a little better. She climbed down from the truck and walked back toward the house. A small boy with a pink-striped T-shirt and shining chestnut hair came up to her and squinted up at her with one eye closed against the sun.

"Is that a space suit?"

"No . . . it's a suit to stop me catching any nasty bugs."

"People got dead in that house."

"I know."

"A little boy got dead."

"Yes. It was very sad."

"Is he still there?"

"No, he's not. He's gone to heaven now."

"When people get dead, you say a prayer."

"That's right. You could say a prayer, couldn't you?"

"I heard a noise in that house."

"Well, it's all over now. Best not to think about it."

The small boy clutched his hands into claws and grimaced like a gargoyle. "I heard a noise like *grrrarrrrrgghhhhhh!*"

"That must have been pretty scary."

"It was the scariest noise in the world. It was *grrrarrrrrgghhhhhh!*"

A young redheaded woman came out of the next-door house and called, "Tyler! What are you doing? You come inside this minute!"

She gave Bonnie a hard, suspicious frown and made a point of waiting in her doorway while the small boy galloped across the front yard. Bonnie was used to it. Nobody liked anything to do with violent death, even if you were just cleaning it up.

Back inside, Esmeralda had finished the vacuuming and was making a start on the walls. They were made of soft, absorbent plaster so it was difficult to leach the bloodstains out completely. There was a diagonal spattering of blood across the bedroom armchair, too, so Bonnie poured some enzyme stain remover on a soft cotton cloth and began to dab it off.

She lifted up the seat cushion and put it on one side. Underneath she saw six or seven brownish, shelllike chrysalises, the same as she had seen in the Glass residence. She picked one of them up and held it to the light. It was translucent, and she could see the shape of the growing larva inside it.

Right in the deepest crevice at the back of the chair, she saw something wriggling. She flicked her cloth at it, so that it dropped out onto the floor. It writhed and twisted on the carpet, because she must have hurt it.

It was another Clouded Apollo caterpillar, exactly like the one she had taken to show Howard Jacobson.

And this was the room where a girl called Maria Carranza had been murdered. With a name like that, she must have been Mexican. Another Mexican connection.

Carefully, Bonnie picked up the caterpillar and two or three of the chrysalises, and dropped them into a plastic bag.

"What's that?" asked Esmeralda, pausing in her scrubbing.

"A caterpillar, the same as the ones we found at the Goodman house."

"What for you want to keep them? They're no good."

"I showed one to Professor Jacobson up at the university. You remember Professor Jacobson? He said they were Mexican."

Esmeralda crossed herself twice and took two or three steps backward.

"What are you so scared of?" Bonnie asked her.

"They're no good. I should kill them. Listen, I fetch the bug spray."

"You know what these are, don't you? Professor Jacobson said they were butterflies, Clouded Apollo butterflies."

"I should kill them."

"Why?"

"Unhealthy, that's all."

"Well, I don't know about unhealthy, but Professor Jacobson said that there was some kind of Mexican goddess called Opsapopalottle or something like that, and that when she wasn't being a goddess she turned herself into one of these butterflies."

"You don't say the name," said Esmeralda, furiously crossing herself again and again.

"Esmeralda we've found these things at three different trauma scenes. You're obviously scared, and I need to know why."

"You don't say the name!" Esmeralda shouted at her. "I don't work for you no more! You don't say the name!"

"Esmeralda, for Christ's sake, will you calm down? These are nothing but caterpillars, but there is a connection."

Esmeralda covered her face with her hands and said nothing for a long time. Bonnie stood beside her waiting for her to recover herself. She kept looking down at the brown rectangular stain on the floor, but now she felt that she could cope with it. If she could find out why David Hinsey had killed Maria Carranza, and why Aaron Goodman had shot his children, and why the Glass family's lives had ended in blood and flies, then maybe she could make sense of her life, and the hideous things that were happening all around her.

Eventually, Esmeralda lowered her hands and said, "You talk to Juan Maderas. He will tell you."

"Who is Juan Maderas?"

"He is a friend of my father. He knows all about the old stories. He knows all about these butterflies."

"Well, how do I get in touch with Juan Maderas?"

"You call me later, three o'clock. Call me at home. I will talk to my father and he will fix it for you to see Juan Maderas."

"And Juan Maderas . . . he knows all about Opsa-popalottle or whatever her name is?"

"Don't say the name! Don't say the name even in fun!"

Bonnie wrapped her arms around Esmeralda and held her close. "I'm sorry, Es. I didn't mean to frighten you. I love you—you know that. Come on, everything's going to be fine. We're going to find out what this is all about, and probably it's all about nothing, but we're going to find out anyhow. Come on, sweetheart. Don't be scared."

"I should kill those things."

"Don't get upset. They're only bugs. Really."

They stayed together for a long time. Bonnie could hear traffic passing along the street outside, and planes taking off from LAX. Esmeralda's hair was wiry and greasy against her cheek, and she smelled of perspiration and cooking fat, but Bonnie kept on holding her for as long as she needed to be held.

RALPH CALLS

They finished cleaning the house by lunchtime. Bonnie was on her way across town to the Riverside waste facility when Ralph called her on her mobile phone.

"Bonnie! Why the hell didn't you say anything?"

"What do you mean? Why didn't I say anything about what?"

"Why didn't you tell me what happened with Phil Cafagna?"

"I don't understand. Nothing happened with Phil Cafagna."

"According to him, it did. He says you made a pass at him, and when he told you he was a married man, you called him all the names under the sun. He's canceled his whole order because of you."

"Ralph, are you kidding? It was Phil Cafagna who

came on to me. He was giving me all kinds of bull-shit about setting me free and stuff like that. And I certainly didn't call him any names. All I said was I wasn't interested."

"He's canceled the order, Bonnie. Don't you under-stand what that means? Pacific takes over sixty per-cent of our production. Without Pacific, we're finished."

"Ralph, I swear to God that I'm telling the truth. He came on to me and wanted me to go to bed with him. I said no, that's all."

"Jesus, Bonnie, it's taken me fifteen years to build up this business."

"Well, doesn't Phil Cafagna have a boss? Call him up and explain what really happened."

"Phil Cafagna's boss is his older brother, Vincent. You think *he'll* believe me? This is the finish, Bonnie. I'm totally sunk."

"Listen, why don't we meet? I have to go to the Riverside waste facility, but then I can change and come right over."

"What's the point?"

"The point is we can work out what to do."

"Forget it, Bonnie. There's nothing we *can* do."

"We can ask Phil Cafagna to reconsider."

"I don't think so. He was upset, Bonnie. I mean he was really, really upset."

"I don't believe this, Ralph. Let me meet you later and we'll talk it over."

"I'm sorry, Bonnie. I have an appointment at the bank. I'll call you tomorrow."

"Ralph—"

"How do you think I feel? You couldn't get anything out of Phil Cafagna, so you chose me as second best. Great. You've done wonders for my ego, believe me, not to mention my faith in women."

"Ralph—I have to talk to you."

"Not now, Bonnie. Go off to your goddamned waste facility."

DUKE CONFESSES

Instead of driving to Riverside, she turned off Washington Boulevard and headed for home. When she parked outside, she heard loud rock music playing from the back of the house. She let herself in, yelling as she did so, "Ray! Do you hear me? Turn that goddamned music down!"

She walked through the kitchen to the yard. There she saw Ray lying on one of the sun loungers, playing air-guitar, his eyes closed. Next to him, reading the newspaper and picking his nose, Duke sat, barechested, with a six-pack of beer beside him.

Bonnie slid back the patio door and stepped outside. She was halfway across the yard before Duke glanced up. He froze, with his finger still halfway up his nose.

"What are you doing here?" Bonnie demanded. "I thought you were starting work today."

"They—uh—they said they didn't need me today. Overstaffed. They sent me home."

"They said they didn't *need* you, on your first day?"

"That's right. . . . It happens sometimes. Business gets slack. They don't need so many people stocking the bar."

"This is the middle of the vacation season and we're talking about the Century Plaza Hotel and business is slack and it's your first day?"

Duke stared at her and obviously didn't know what to say. On the next sun lounger, Ray had suddenly become aware that she was there and opened his eyes.

"Duke," said Bonnie, "I can think of two possible options here. The first is that you're telling me the truth, in which case I'll call your boss at the Century Plaza and check it out. The second is that you're lying, which will save me the trouble."

Duke looked over at Ray, but all Ray could do was shrug. In the end, he looked back at Bonnie and said, "Save yourself the trouble."

"Okay, you're lying. So I can think of two further options here. The first is that you haven't shown up for work without bothering to tell your boss, in which case I'll call him and make an excuse that you're sick. The second is that you don't have a job at the Century Plaza at all—that you never made even the slightest attempt to get one—in which case I don't have to make the phone call at all, do I? I can save myself even *more* trouble."

Duke chewed over this for nearly half a minute. Then he said, "Yeah."

"Yeah what, Duke?"

"Yeah, save yourself even more trouble."

She called Esmeralda shortly after three. Esmeralda said, "Everything's arranged. Come downtown and see us at eight o'clock."

"Okay, I'll be there."

"You don't sound so good. Is everything okay?"

She turned to look at Duke and Ray, still sprawled on their sun loungers out in the yard and said, "Sure. I can manage. I'll see you later."

THE MYSTIC

Esmeralda lived in a seven-story apartment building on Sixteenth Street only a block away from the Santa Monica Freeway. It was a brown brick edifice that stood on its own between two rubble-strewn demolition sites. Outside, children were playing in a dilapidated Mercury Marquis with no windows in it.

At 7:56 P.M., Bonnie parked Duke's Buick next to the Mercury and climbed out. She checked her lipstick and primped her spray-stiffened hair with her fingers. The traffic noise here was tremendous, and there was an eye-watering tang of exhaust fumes in the air. She climbed up the steps to the front door, which was already half open. It was freshly painted in glossy maroon, and inside Bonnie could see a green linoleum floor that had been polished to a high shine. She pressed the door buzzer for apartment four, and a man's voice said, "*Quién?*"

"It's Bonnie Winter. I'm looking for Esmeralda."

"*Sí*, Esmeralda's here. Come on up."

She walked along the corridor until she reached the elevator. One of the apartment doors was open, and she could see a young woman standing in front of a mirror fixing combs in her hair. A TV was tuned to a Spanish-language comedy program, and the young woman was smiling at herself.

Bonnie went up to the fourth floor. The elevator was cramped and slow and smelled of Lysol, but somebody had tried to make it more cheerful by pasting postcards of Mexico on the walls and varnishing them.

Esmeralda was waiting for her outside the elevator. She was wearing a crimson satin dress that Bonnie had never seen before, and there was a crimson ribbon in her hair. "Juan is already here," she said, in a hushed voice.

She ushered Bonnie into a small living room that was filled with oversize 1950s furniture—a chocolate-brown couch with white lace antimacassars on the back, two chocolate-brown armchairs with tapestry cushion covers, a circular table with a brown fringed velveteen tablecloth. In one corner stood a glass-fronted display cabinet crammed with china and ornaments, and the fireplace looked like the altar of a Catholic cathedral, with a plaster figure of the Virgin Mary, candles, rosaries and luminous plastic grottoes.

In one of the armchairs sat Esmeralda's father, whom Bonnie had met several times before. He was a shy man with curly gray hair, a large gray mustache and an intensely white shirt. In the other armchair sat a thin, almost emaciated man of about forty-five with acne-pitted cheeks and hooded eyes. He was handsome in a ravaged way, with slicked-back black hair and chiseled sideburns. He wore a black shirt with a silver bolo necktie and a black suit with a narrow waist and very wide lapels.

"Bonnie, this is Juan Maderas."

Juan stood up and took both of Bonnie's hands. He was very tall, at least six foot three inches, and he was wearing some floral cologne that immediately took her off her guard because it reminded her so much of the camellias that had been laid on her father's casket. "Esmeralda has told me about you," he said, in a deep, hoarse voice. "It seems as if you are somebody very special. The job that you do, that takes somebody very special."

"I just do my best," said Bonnie. "Thanks for taking the trouble to see me."

"No, no. No trouble. I was very interested when Esmeralda told me about the butterflies. Very interested."

"I never saw anything like them before, and I've seen just about every creepy-crawly that there is. In my business, you get to be an amateur expert on bugs."

"Why don't you sit down?" suggested Esmeralda's father. "Esmeralda, open some wine."

"I never drink and drive, thanks," said Bonnie.

"Coca-Cola, maybe?"

"Watching my figure. Water would be fine."

She sat down on the couch next to Esmeralda's

father. Juan Maderas sat down, too, and laced his long fingers together. On his right middle finger he wore a silver ring with a skull on it. "Esmeralda said that you took the butterflies to a professor at UCLA."

"Howard Jacobson. Yes, he's the best. He's written all kinds of books on bugs and forensics. Often it's the only way that you can tell how long somebody's been dead, by the life cycle of the flies that infest their body, having regard to the ambient temperature and all. People go off real quick in a heatwave—you'd be surprised."

"And this Professor Jacobson was sure that the butterfly was the Clouded Apollo?"

"That's right. And he told me about the legend, too. The demon goddess whose name I can't pronounce too good."

"Itzpapalotl," said Juan Maderas. "Her name translated means 'obsidian butterfly.' That was because she had broad butterfly wings sprouting from her shoulders, with the blades of sharp obsidian knives all the way around the edges."

"That's what Howard told me. He said she had a knife for a tongue, too."

"That's right. Itzpapalotl fell from heaven, along with the Tzitzimime, who dropped from the sky in a tremendous variety of shapes, such as scorpions, or toads, or even walking sticks. We call them 'deadly things.' There was one Tzitzimime which took on the form of a donkey's skull, and it would appear at crossroads at night. If you saw it, it would follow you all the way home, screaming."

Juan Maderas took another sip of wine, and then he said, "Itzpapalotl sometimes wore an invisible cloak so that nobody could see her. At other times she dressed up as a lady of the Mexican court, caking her face with white powder and lining her cheeks with strips of rubber. Her fingers tapered into the claws of a jaguar, and her toes into eagle's claws.

"On certain days of the Aztec calendar, she would fly like a butterfly through the towns and villages with scores of dead witches, also butterflies, swarming behind her. They would enter people's houses and settle in their ears, whispering evil words to them, persuading them to murder their wives and their children. Itzpapalotl wanted more spirits in Mictlampa with her, even more butterflies, and the most loyal spirits were those who had loved their families dearly but had turned on them, and killed them."

"That's it," Bonnie nodded. "They killed the people they loved the most. That's exactly what happened in all of the three cases where I discovered these butterflies."

Juan Maderas stared at Bonnie, and his hooded black eyes glittered like beetles. "Can you really believe, in the twenty-first century, that these people were murdered by an ancient Aztec demon?"

"I don't know. It sounds crazy, doesn't it? It really sounds crazy. But none of these people seemed to have much of a motive . . . not for killing their children, anyhow. One family was having problems over child custody, and one family was full of druggies, but the other family . . . Everybody said the father was such a good father, but he shot his three kids for no obvious reason at all."

"Sometimes people do that kind of thing. You

should know that better than anybody. It doesn't
mean that they've been encouraged to do it by
Itzpapalotl."

"But the only common elements between these
three trauma scenes were the butterflies and some kind
of Mexican connection. I don't suppose the Mexican
connection would mean much, normally, but Howard said that the Clouded Apollo butterfly is never
found here in California. Never."

Juan Maderas was silent for a long time. He sipped
his wine again, then took out a black silk handkerchief to wipe his lips. "I don't know what to say to
you. There are many who still believe in Itzpapalotl
and Micantecutli, the great lord of hell, and the Tzitzimime. I saw some old men when I was younger,
friends of my father's, who drew blood out of their
noses and their ears and dripped it over walking
sticks to keep away the evil spirits that they believed
were concealed inside them. But these days, I'm not
so sure."

"What did people do to keep Itzpapalotl away?"

"They sacrificed people, usually, cut their hearts
out, and they would sing her a flattering song, calling
her their mother and their protector."

"And it worked?"

"According to the picture writing, yes. The Aztec
priests kept extraordinarily detailed records of everything they did, every sacrifice they made."

Bonnie thought for a while. But then she said, "I'm
a very practical woman, Mr. Maderas. I've seen a lot
of dead people, and I don't believe in ghosts. But
something's happening here, something very strange,
and there has to be a reason for it."

"Well . . . you may be right. The Mexican people suffer many injustices in Los Angeles, and a great deal of prejudice. Perhaps Itzpapalotl has come back from hell to start some kind of crusade on their behalf."

Esmeralda's father suddenly cleared his throat and said, "When I was young, the man who ran our local store insulted my mother. They found his body in Griffith Park, with his tongue cut out. That was the way that Xipe Totec, the night drinker, used to kill his victims . . . cut out their tongues so that they bled to death, and drink it."

"They never found who killed him?"

"How could they? It was Xipe Totec."

Bonnie stayed a little while longer, but she was very unsettled. She couldn't decide if Juan Maderas really believed in Itzpapalotl, or if he was humoring her. His tone of voice was dry and monotonous and matter-of-fact, as if they were discussing the price of candles, yet there was something sly about him, too. Occasionally Esmeralda's father would interject some odd non sequitur, such as, "You mustn't sleep in hell. . . . You must keep awake to endure your punishment. . . . That's what they say."

Bonnie left the apartment building feeling confused and depressed. She thought of calling Ralph at home, but then she decided that it would probably make him even angrier with her than he was already. She had felt so elated after spending the night with him in Pasadena, especially after her humiliation at Kyle Lennox's party. She had really felt that her life was going to change. She hadn't allowed herself to consider the possibility that she might have actually left Duke and gone to live with Ralph instead; but she hadn't been more than one step away from it.

She played "Evergreen" on the car stereo as she drove back home. She sang along, and suddenly the tears burst out of her eyes and ran down her cheeks and dripped onto her new stonewashed jeans. She couldn't bear the thought that Ralph might never make love to her again.

Up ahead of her, the traffic signals danced red and blurry and bright, like lamps at a Mexican carnival.

An Unusual Silence

When Bonnie opened her eyes the next morning, the first thing that struck her was the silence. She lay in bed looking up at the ceiling. There was a hairline crack in the plaster which had always reminded her of a witch, with a pointed nose and a pointed chin. The sun shivered across her face and made her look as if she were winking her eye. After a little while she sat up and checked the bedside clock. It was 8:23 A.M.

She sat up, horrified. Duke was going to be late for work and Ray was going to be late for school and she was going to be late for—

Then she suddenly realized. None of them was going to be late for anything. Duke didn't really have a job and Ray wasn't going to school and she didn't

have a job to go to, either—not unless Ralph changed
his mind about Phil Cafagna.

She prodded the bundle of sheets next to her.
"Duke—it's almost eight-thirty. You want some
coffee?"

He didn't answer, but then, she didn't expect him
to. You could have crashed a 747 right outside the
house and he wouldn't have woken up. She prodded
him again. "Do you want some coffee? I'm not cooking you anything this morning. I wouldn't want you
to accuse me of murdering you."

Still he didn't answer. Exasperated, she said,
"Come on, Duke, you're not lying in bed all day.
You're going out to find yourself a job."

She took hold of the sheets and dragged them off
him. Except that he wasn't there. The shape that she
had thought was Duke was simply the extra pillows
that she must have discarded in the heat of the night.

She frowned, and stood up, and padded across the
pale blue nylon-carpeted floor. "Duke?" she called,
opening the bathroom door. No Duke—and for the
first time ever in the history of the Winter marriage,
the toilet seat was down.

She went through to the living room. Sometimes
Duke got so drunk that he fell asleep on the couch
in front of the television. But the television was
switched off, there was nobody lying on the couch,
and the cushions were all straightened. This was
very weird.

"*Duke?*" she said, but this time she spoke so softly
that he wouldn't have been able to hear her.

He wasn't in the kitchen. She even opened the larder. He wasn't in the yard, either—and thank God, his body wasn't floating in the pool. She saw herself frowning in the gilt-framed mirror in the hallway as she went back to see if he had dropped off in Ray's room—although why he should do that, she couldn't think. He always called it The Funkatorium. She could almost hear him now. "Kids today, you know why they fart so much? It's the food. All those god-damned vegetables. How can they call that health food when it practically asphyxiates you?"

She knocked on Ray's door and said, "Ray? Is your father in with you?"

There was no answer, so she knocked again and looked around the door. There was no Duke lying on the carpet, but then, there was no Ray lying in the bed, either. The bed was tidy, and the drapes weren't even drawn.

Bonnie was becoming seriously worried now. She remembered going to bed last night. She remembered taking a long shower and putting on her nightgown and climbing into bed. She remembered wondering how long it would take for Duke to come to bed, because when he did he almost always woke her up, cursing and burping and falling over his feet. But that was all. She couldn't remember kissing Ray good night, the way she usually did.

She went to the front door. It was locked and bolted from the inside and the chain was on. The patio door at the back was safety-bolted, too. None of the windows were open, and they all had locks. So Duke and Ray must have left the house before she went to bed, and she must have locked all the doors after them. Yet she couldn't remember doing

it, and she couldn't think why Duke and Ray would
have gone. Duke had hardly any money, so it was
doubtful that they would have gone to a hotel; and
Duke had hardly any friends, either. Maybe they had
spent the night with one of Ray's buddies.

But why? She could remember arguing with Duke
because he had lied to her about finding a job. She
remembered Ray saying something about cheap
Mexican labor ruining their lives, and Mexican drug
traffickers killing one of his friends. But that had
been early in the afternoon. She simply couldn't remember what had happened next.

Oh, yes. She had called Esmeralda at three o'clock,
and showered, and changed, and gone down to Sixteenth Street to see her. And talked to Juan Maderas.
And then come home again. But had Duke and Ray
been at home when she got back? They couldn't have
gone far, because she had borrowed Duke's car—
which was still parked next to her truck in the driveway outside.

She felt as if she had been to a very drunken party
the night before and simply couldn't piece things
together.

She went into the kitchen again and poured herself
a glass of orange juice. When she had finished it, she
drank some more straight out of the carton. There
was no sign of a serious fight. Nothing broken, so
far as she could see. In fact, the house was immaculate. Even the carpets had been vacuum cleaned and
the pile raked up with a carpet rake.

She went back to Ray's room and found his Bart
Simpson phone book. Most of the pages were
crowded with scribbles and cartoons and exclamation

points, but she managed to find the number of his closest friend, Kendal.

"Mrs. Rakusen? It's Bonnie Winter. I'm sorry if I've disturbed you, but I was wondering if you'd seen anything of Ray. No? He didn't ask to stay with you last night or anything? I see. Well, could you ask Kendal? Okay. Well, if you do hear from him, can you ask him to call his mother? He didn't come home last night, and I'm a little worried about him. Well, yes, after that last business. Thanks."

She called two more friends she could think of, and a girl he used to go out with called Cherry-Jo. None of them had seen him or heard from Ray.

She sat in the living room biting her lip and wondering what to do. She took another look all around the house, even bending down and looking under the beds.

At last she called Ruth.

"Ruth . . . something weird has happened."

"Don't tell me that you and Duke have actually—you know—"

"I'm not kidding, Ruth. Duke and Ray have both disappeared."

"Hey, congratulations! How did you manage it?"

"They've gone, Ruth, and I don't know how and I don't know where."

"Hey, you're serious, aren't you? What do you mean, they've disappeared?"

Bonnie told her everything about her argument with Duke, and all about the empty beds and the toilet seat down and the doors locked on the inside. "They must have gone, but I don't remember them going. It's like a blank. It's like they never even existed."

"Nah," said Ruth, dismissively. "I think they're pulling some kind of stupid stunt. Duke's the kind of guy who hates it when a woman tells him what to do, especially when it comes to getting his butt off the couch and earning himself a living. They'll show up, believe me, as soon as their guts start growling."

Bonnie was about to tell Ruth about her visit to Esmeralda's house yesterday evening, and Juan Maderas, and Itzpapalotl, but then she decided against it. She didn't want her to think that she was totally bananas.

BONNIE CALLS RALPH

"Ralph, you have to—*crackle*—that I didn't come on to Phil Cafagna." The connection kept breaking up.

"Don't worry about it. It's forgotten."

"But I don't want it to be forgotten. What happened between us was something—*crackle*."

"I know. I'm not saying it wasn't. But Glamorex is falling apart, Bonnie, and I don't have the time to think about anything but saving it."

"Ralph, Duke's left me."

"What?"

"He's left me. I don't know where he's gone, but he's taken Ray, too."

"I'm sorry, Bonnie. It doesn't make any difference if Duke's left you. It wouldn't make any difference if Vanessa dropped dead. There are times when things work out and there are times when they don't. Call it fate. Call it what you like."

"Ralph, I'm actually pleading with you. What you gave me—you showed me that a man could— *crackle*—for me. I've never felt that before. Never. And don't tell me you didn't like what I did for you."

There was a pause so long that Bonnie felt her heartbeat twenty times. Then Ralph said, "I love you, Bonnie. I'm sorry if I hurt you. I'm hurting, too. But we both have to accept that it's just one of those might-have-beens, isn't it?"

"No, Ralph! Listen, Ralph—"

But then she stopped herself, because she knew that it was no use, and that she never got lucky like this. She didn't switch the phone off, but slowly lowered it and stood in the street right opposite the Glamorex building looking up at Ralph's office, where she could see him standing next to the window. After a while he hung up his phone. Then he stood with his arms tightly folded and his head bent, like somebody suffering from agonizing chest pain.

BUTTERFLY

When she returned home, she called more of Ray's friends, but none of them had seen him. She even called up Duke's elderly mother, who lived in a nursing home in Anaheim. All Mrs. Winter did was mumble and cough and ask her repeatedly to remind her who she was. "Bonnie who? Duke? Who wants to know?"

She called her own mother, too, who made the nearest noise that Bonnie had ever heard to an audible shrug. "*Pwoff*, that's what men are like. They leave you when you least expect it. I never could tell what you saw in him anyhow."

She searched the house for anything that could give her a clue to what might have happened. Behind the water heater she found a copy of *Hustler*, corrugated with damp. She found a lock-knife under Ray's pajamas, and a twist of kitchen foil with a minuscule amount of marijuana in it. But nothing that explained how and why they might have disappeared.

Ruth called. "Any sign of the wandering boys yet?"

"Nothing. I can't work out what's happened to them."

"They didn't say anything before they left?"

"I don't remember them leaving."

"That was only yesterday. How can you not remember them leaving?"

"I just can't, that's all. We had an argument. Maybe they walked out then."

"You know what you need? You need a break. Why don't you come on over to my place and we'll have a couple of drinks and polish our toenails."

"Ruth, I'm really worried."

While she was talking to Ruth, her eye suddenly caught a movement on the potted plant on the windowsill. A slow, humping movement, like a caterpillar.

"Hold on, Ruth. Just hold on a minute."

She carefully laid down the receiver and walked across to the window. With the tip of the ballpoint pen she was holding in her hand, she carefully lifted up the leaves of the plant, one by one. And there, underneath the third leaf, was the black spotted larva of *Parnassius mnemonsyne*, the butterfly known as Clouded Apollo, or Itzpapalotl.

Bonnie stared at the caterpillar and didn't know what to do. On the table behind her, she could hear Ruth saying in a shrunken voice, *"Hello? Hello? Bonnie—are you there? What's wrong?"*

She let the leaf fall back and returned to the phone. "Ruth . . . I'm beginning to think that something dreadful might have happened."

"Come on, Bonnie . . . you know Duke. He'll be back before you know it."

"I think I have to talk to Dan Munoz. I really think that something dreadful might have happened."

Dan came around an hour and a half later. He was wearing a cream blazer with gold buttons and a black silk shirt.

"Hi, Bonnie, how's it going?"

She let him into the living room. "You want a cup of coffee or something?"

"No, thanks. I was supposed to be over on La Brea about fifteen minutes ago. Some kid stabbed his best friend through the heart with the pointy end of a beach umbrella."

"I wouldn't have bothered you, but I'm really worried."

"Hey, that's okay. What are friends for?"

She handed him a small glass screw-top jar. "I found this crawling up that plant over there."

Dan held it up and peered at it, his eye magnified by the glass. "Ugly little dude, ain't he?"

"It's the same kind of butterfly that I was telling you about . . . the Clouded Apollo."

"Yes? And?"

"And Duke and Ray have both disappeared, and I think that something terrible must have happened."

Dan looked around the living room. "Something terrible like—what?"

"Well, suppose that thing *is* some kind of a Mexi-

can demon goddess—supposing she looks like a butterfly by day, but when it gets dark she turns into
this insect monster with knives on her wings?"

Dan opened his jaw wide and thoughtfully rubbed
his chin. "Oka-a-ay . . . suppose she does?"

"She could have killed them . . . and then she
could have taken them away."

"If she killed them, where's the blood? She's got
knives on her wings, right? And a knife for a tongue?
There would have been catsup all over. But this place
looks like a centerfold for *Ideal Homes*."

"Maybe she just took them away."

"No sign of a struggle? And you didn't even notice? Come on, Bonnie!"

"I don't know. I can't seem to remember. It's like
there's a whole chunk of yesterday just missing."

"You were overtired, probably. I get that, too,
lapses of memory when I'm tired. I get lapses of
memory when I'm *not* tired. The best thing to do is
go back over everything you did yesterday, like, step
by step in chronological order."

"I've tried to. I still can't remember."

"What did you do? You cleaned up George Keighley's house in the morning—what time did you finish
up there?"

"Twelve, twelve-fifteen, something like that."

"Then what? You dumped the mattresses at the
Riverside waste facility?"

"Yes. Then I came home, and Ray was here but so
was Duke. The thing is that Duke was supposed to
be working. He said he'd found a job at the Century
Plaza, but that was just a lie. We had an argument
about it."

"Did he walk out then?"

"No . . . I called Esmeralda at about three o'clock, and I remember looking out into the yard when I was making the call and they were both still lying on their loungers. I showered and changed, and about quarter after seven I went downtown to meet Esmeralda and her father and this guy called Juan Maderas, who knows all about Mexican mythology and stuff."

"Then you came home?"

"That's right."

"What time was that, when you came home?"

"I don't know. Not too late. Nine-thirty, maybe."

"Were Duke and Ray still here when you came home?"

Bonnie frowned. She remembered parking the Buick. She remembered opening the front door. Then all she could remember was climbing into bed and saying, "Good night, Duke. Sleep tight. Mind the bugs don't bite." If she had spoken to him, he *must* have been there.

"Duke was there," she said, nodding slowly at first and then more vigorously. "Duke was definitely there. He must have drunk too much beer and gone to bed early."

"How about Ray?"

She had knocked on Ray's bedroom door and called out, "Good night, Ray . . . don't go listening to those earphones all night." So Ray must have been there, too.

"Yes . . . Ray was there."

Dan grimaced. "You know what this leaves us with, don't you? Sometime in the middle of the night, Duke and Ray left their beds and disappeared out the front door, miraculously locking and chaining it behind them."

"That's why I think that something terrible's happened."

"You realize you're talking supernatural here. Like, *X-Files*. You don't really believe that, do you?"

"I don't know. Ask Howard Jacobson. Ask this Juan Maderas character. Ask Esmeralda's father. *They* all seem to think that this insect goddess really exists."

Dan took out his notebook and flipped it open. "I'll tell you what I'm going to do here, Bonnie. Once they've finished up on La Brea, I'm going to ask a couple of the forensics guys to swing over this way and give this house a quick once-over. That's if you have no objections."

"Of course not, if they can find out what happened to Duke and Ray."

"Well, I'm not making any promises, but you never know. Meanwhile, you should keep on phoning around. Check up on any bars that Duke might go to. Ask his friends if they've seen him."

"He doesn't have any friends."

Life Without Duke

The next four days went past like a silent movie. Every morning she woke up and the house was silent. She sat at the kitchen table and ate a yogurt, watching the television with the sound on mute. Then she stood in the living room, staring out of the window, expecting at any minute to see Duke and Ray walking across the street, laughing and waving. But they never did.

In the afternoons, when the sun came around the house, she went out into the yard and flicked through magazines, although all the time she was waiting for the phone to ring. When it did, she invariably jumped and felt a sharp salt taste in her mouth.

On the fifth day she had just finished her yogurt when Lieutenant Munoz called her. "Listen, sweet cheeks, there's a cleaning job in Benedict Canyon you might be interested in. Do you want to meet me there—say, around ten?"

"I don't know, Dan."

"This is going to need your delicate touch, Bonnie. I'm sure that Ken Kessler could clean up just as good as you, technically. He's willing to do it if you're not interested. But . . . you'll see what I mean when you get here."

"Okay . . . I guess it's not doing me any good, sitting around the house and moping."

"That's my girl. See you later, okay?"

She had never seen so much blood in her life. It hardly seem possible that one human being could contain so much of it, let alone crawl around a whole house from room to room bleeding so profusely.

The house was down at the bottom of a sharp slope on the east side of Benedict Canyon—a smart, single-story residence with white-painted walls and bougainvillea sprawling over the porch. Inside, it was fiercely air-conditioned and totally white, so that it felt like the inside of an igloo. The walls were white, the carpets were white, the furniture was white. That was what made the trails of blood look even grislier.

There were splatters of blood, loops of blood, Jackson Pollock action paintings of blood. There was blood on the walls, blood on the furniture, blood on the refrigerator door. The whole nine pints.

Dan took Bonnie into the living room first. "I'll tell you what happened. Mrs. Chloris Neighbor went to a regular dance class every Thursday afternoon, for three hours. Her husband, Mr. Anthony Neighbor, worked at home as a freelance architect, so on Thursday afternoon he was guaranteed some time on his own.

"Last Thursday afternoon he celebrated his few hours of freedom by taking off all of his clothes and watching a pornographic videotape. Sometime during the course of this entertainment, he decided to increase his pleasure by inserting a fluorescent light tube into his rectum. He must have grown more and more excited, because he then decided to switch the light tube on. Whereupon it shattered and caused massive internal slicing.

"This is only surmise, but it seems to us that he was too embarrassed to call 911. He crawled from room to room, trying to find a way to stem the bleeding, but in the end he collapsed and died. This was what Mrs. Neighbor had to come home to."

Bonnie rubbed the toe of her shoe into the carpet. "This is going to cost."

"Mrs. Neighbor's outside if you want to talk to her."

"Okay."

They went outside. Mrs. Neighbor was standing under the trees, her face lit up by the sunlight that danced through the leaves. She was small, very thin, with an ash-blond bob and big, haunted eyes. She wore a black silk cheongsam, and she looked more like a frightened little animal than a woman.

"Mrs. Neighbor, I'm Bonnie Winter. I'm sorry for your loss."

"Thank you. It's very hard to understand, losing your husband like that."

"I know."

"It makes me feel—well, I guess you can imagine how it makes me feel. Inadequate. If I'd been adequate, he never would have—"

"You can't blame yourself, Mrs. Neighbor. Who knows what goes on in the minds of men?"

She glanced quickly at Dan, as if daring him to say, "*Only The Shadow knows, ho-ho-ho.*"

Mrs. Neighbor said, "I couldn't clean the blood up myself. It's his precious blood. I worshiped him. I worshiped every hair on his head. I never thought that I would have to mop up his blood from the floor. I couldn't. That's like mopping up his life, mopping up our life together."

"Do you happen to know if you're insured for trauma damage?"

Mrs. Neighbor stared at her wide-eyed. "What?"

"Your late husband left a very expensive mess, Mrs. Neighbor."

"That's his lifeblood in there. That's *him*."

"Yes," said Bonnie. "And I promise you that we can clean it all up with really great respect." Not to mention Lysol.

As she walked back to the Buick, Dan came over and opened the door for her.

"I had a report back from forensics this morning."

"Oh, yes?"

"They checked your house over pretty good. And do you know what they said? They said it was the cleanest house they had ever had the misfortune to come across. Spotless."

"Nothing to give them any clue what might have happened to Duke and Ray?"

"Nothing at all. They even checked the handles of the kitchen knives."

"Why would they do that?"

"Kitchen knives are the most commonly used weapon in domestic homicide, that's why. Most perpetrators wash the knives afterward, but what they don't realize is that if you stab somebody hard, microscopic traces of human blood tend to penetrate the crevices between the steel blade and the wooden or plastic handle, and they're almost impossible to get rid of . . . just like microscopic traces of meat or cheese will always penetrate those same crevices, and be just as difficult to remove, even in a dishwasher using a biological detergent."

"So? What are you trying to tell me?"

"I'm trying to tell you that one of your kitchen knives wasn't new, but it was as clean as new. In other words, it contained no trace of any biological waste matter whatsoever. You can only get a knife *that* clean by soaking it in enzyme solutions specifically formulated to digest cream, yogurt, milk, egg, ice cream, cheese and blood."

"I don't understand."

"Nobody's drawing any inferences, Bonnie. Nobody's making any accusations. We're simply telling you that one of your kitchen knives was unnaturally clean. That's not evidence, I'll admit—but it's an interesting *lack* of evidence."

"That's all they found out?"

"They'd like to make a more detailed search, if you'll allow it. But as your friend, I'd probably say that you ought to talk to your lawyer before you let them back into your house a second time."

"This knife thing—what are you trying to say, Dan? You're trying to tell me that I stabbed them to death or something?"

"Bonnie, sweetheart—nobody's saying nothing."

"You're warning me, aren't you? You think they're dead, and you're warning me that I'm one of your suspects! Come on, Dan, this is me you're talking to!"

"We don't have any evidence of any kind that Duke and Ray are dead. It's kind of mysterious that they should both have disappeared without taking any clothes or personal possessions. But stranger things happen. People are disappearing all the time. Some of them don't even take their shoes."

Bonnie sat down behind the driver's seat and started the engine. "Something very weird happened in my house, Dan. I know you don't believe all this stuff about the butterflies, but I think you're making a very big mistake. The butterflies . . . they're the key to this whole thing."

Dan closed the car door for her. "You going to do this job?" he asked, nodding toward the Neighbor residence.

"Oh, sure. I've got plenty of enzyme solution for getting rid of blood."

"Bonnie—"

"What? You're not going to ask me out to dinner, are you?"

"No," said Dan, shaking his head. "I was just going to say . . . nothing important." He patted the roof of the car, stepped back and watched her drive away in a cloud of oily blue smoke.

THE MYSTIC EATS GORDITAS

She met him at Nopales, the Mexican restaurant on Pico Boulevard. He was sitting in a corner way in the back of the restaurant, and she didn't see him at first. The place was crowded and noisy, and a five-piece Mexican band was playing guitars and trumpets and bongos on a tiny stage.

At last she caught hold of a waiter and said, "Juan Maderas?"

"In back. Table twenty-one."

He stood up as she approached him and drew out a chair for her. He was still dressed in black, although his bolo had given way to a florid black scarf.

"You found it okay?"

"I took a taxi."

He sat down and offered her the bottle of red wine, but she said, "No—no, thanks. And listen, don't let me stop you eating. Whatever that is, it looks delicious."

"Gorditas," he said. "That means 'little fat ones.' Little cups made out of tortilla dough, deep fried and filled with mashed beans and shredded meat."

"My husband would never let me eat Mexican."

"Your husband has disappeared."

She nodded. "My son, too. It's like one of those locked-room mysteries, you know?"

"I don't think it's a locked-room mystery. I think it's a locked-mind mystery."

"Well, you're right, in a way. I'm finding it very hard to remember what happened that afternoon. I don't recall Duke and Ray actually leaving . . . and they were home when I came back from seeing you. But in the morning they were both gone, and all of the doors and windows were locked."

"So what do you think happened?"

"I don't know. That's why I wanted to talk to you."

"Why me? I'm not a policeman, or a psychiatrist. I'm a writer, that's all. A historian."

Bonnie opened her bag and took out the screw-top jar. "I found this in my living room."

"A Clouded Apollo. I see. So you think that Itzpapalotl had something to do with your husband and son's disappearance?"

Bonnie nodded. "I think she could have."

"How?"

"Well, I don't exactly know when they disappeared. But if it was nighttime, Itzpapalotl could have transformed herself, couldn't she? Instead of being a butterfly, she could have turned herself into an insect monster, the way you described her, with knives on her wings and everything. She could have killed them and turned *them* into butterflies, too, like the witches in the legend, and that's how they disappeared. When I opened the front door, they simply flew away."

"And you believe that this could actually have happened?"

"How else could they have gotten out of the house without my seeing them?"

"But Itzpapalotl would have had to kill them to turn them into butterflies. Only a person who is dead and damned can become a Clouded Apollo. And if she did kill them, what happened to the blood? In Aztec sacrifices, the heart is cut beating out of the rib cage and held up for everybody to see. If that had happened, surely your house would have looked like a slaughterhouse."

"Yes," said Bonnie.

"But there was no blood, as I understand it."

"No."

Bonnie was silent for a moment. Juan Maderas calmly watched her, forking up his gorditas. The band began to play a slow, sad, quavering song, the musical equivalent of somebody's lower lip trembling.

After a while, Bonnie said, "I had another idea, too."

"Go on."

"Supposing Itzpapalotl came into my house that afternoon—in daylight—disguised as a butterfly."

"Yes. That's how she conceals herself."

"Supposing she settled on my ear and whispered that I should—well, supposing she suggested to me that I should get rid of the people I love the most. And I didn't realize that she'd done it. I mean, whispered to me like that.

"Supposing I took it into my head that I had to kill Duke and Ray. Without even realizing that it was Itzpapalotl who wanted me to do it. Because a whole piece of that afternoon is just missing, you know? Like a lost piece of jigsaw puzzle."

"So you think it's conceivable that Itzpapalotl persuaded you to murder Duke and Ray yourself?"

"I don't know. It's insane, isn't it? But where did they go?"

"That's precisely the flaw in your second theory, isn't it? Let's say that you're right, and that Itzpapalotl *did* cajole you into killing Duke and Ray. . . . How did you do it? Did you strangle them? Remember there were two of them, and you would have had to strangle them one at a time. And what would you strangle them with? Your bare hands? Did you stab them? The same thing applies. . . . You couldn't have killed them both at once. And besides, there was no blood. You could have shot them, I suppose."

"We don't own a gun. Well, we did, but Duke sold it."

"That eliminates *that* possibility, then. But more than anything else, where did they go, even if you killed them? How does a woman dispose of the bodies of two men from a suburban house without anybody seeing her do it? And where are the bodies now? They haven't been found, have they?"

Bonnie brushed back her hair with her hand. "I came to see you because I thought you could give me some kind of explanation."

"You mean you thought you could lay the blame for what happened to your husband and son on a Mexican demon goddess?"

"Don't you believe in her?"

"Of course I believe in her. But I also believe that ancient demons can't do very much in the modern world unless they're called on."

"You think that I *summoned* her?"

"It's possible. Perhaps you don't remember doing it. Perhaps you do, but you're pretending that you don't."

The band struck up a dreamy version of *"La Pesadilla."* Bonnie said, "You don't think it was me, though, do you? If somebody's murdered them, it wasn't me. I mean, even if it was me, I didn't know what I was doing. It was Itzpapalotl."

"Only you can know that."

THE DAY OF THE CLOUDED APOLLO

She stood in the living room, her bleached-blond hair shining in the afternoon sunlight. She was staring at a large reproduction of a painting of Elvis that Duke had given her for her thirtieth birthday. It was Elvis in *Love Me Tender*, with his cowboy hat and his buckskin fringes.

She remembered that birthday so vividly. Duke had been working then, and he had taken her out to a country-and-western restaurant for steak and ribs and dancing. They had laughed so much that Duke had been forced to pull onto the side of the road.

He had put his arms around her and kissed her and said, "You and me, we're forever—do you know that? Till death us do fucking part."

Carefully, she lifted the picture down from the wall. Then she propped it up against the couch and unscrewed the metal eyes at the back. Carrying the picture wire, she went to the kitchen and took her gardening gloves out of the drawer, and put them on.

Outside, on the patio, Ray was lying back on the sun lounger, his eyes closed, his music playing just as loud as before. Duke was reading the sports pages and starting on another beer.

She slid open the patio door. Ray's music was so deafening that neither of them looked up. She stepped out onto the patio and stood behind Duke's sun lounger for almost half a minute, not moving, the picture wire held behind her back. Duke probably knew she was there, but he didn't acknowledge her. He was sulking because she had discovered that he had been lying about the job at the Century Plaza.

Bonnie thought: *If you look up and smile at me, you'll probably live.* But all he did was turn the page of the sports section and take another swig from his can of beer.

She was a strong woman. All that scrubbing, all that bed carrying, all that vacuuming. She whipped the picture wire over his head and around his neck, and she pulled it tight before he had the chance to get his fingers underneath it. He twisted and kicked and bounced himself up and down in an effort to get free, but Bonnie pulled tighter and tighter until the wire had disappeared into the flesh of his neck and blood was running down his shoulders.

She kept the picture wire tight until Duke gave a small, convulsive shudder, and his head dropped sideways. All this time, Ray hadn't opened his eyes once.

She unwound the picture wire and walked around

to Ray's sun lounger. He was singing silently to himself and popping his fingers. She bent over him and kissed his forehead.

Open your eyes, she thought. *Look at me. See me for what I am. Then I will spare you.* But Ray simply grinned and kept on silently singing and finger popping.

Afterward, she went into the living room and phoned Esmeralda.

Esmeralda said, "Everything's arranged. Come downtown to see us at eight o'clock."

"Okay, I'll be there."

"You don't sound so good. Is everything okay?"

"Sure. I can manage. I'll see you later."

She looked out of the window, and she could still see Duke and Ray sprawled on their sun loungers.

THE JIGSAW

Bonnie woke up with a start. The first thing she did was reach out to feel if Duke was lying beside her, but he wasn't. It was still early, 5:17 A.M., and the sky was the color of faded blue flowers.

She got out of bed and went to the bathroom. She looked at herself in the mirror, her hair all wild, her eyes puffy. She scarcely recognized herself. She could have been one of those old women you see sleeping rough in Echo Park.

That scene out on the patio, with Duke and Ray— that hadn't really happened, had it? It couldn't have. It had been a nightmare, that's all. She couldn't have garroted her own husband and her own son. As Juan Maderas had commented—if she *had* killed them, where were the bodies?

All the same, she found it impossible to go back

to sleep. She went into the kitchen and drank a big swig of freezing-cold orange juice. Then she stood by the window with her palate aching, staring out at the empty sun loungers. She remembered seeing Duke and Ray all sprawled out on them while she phoned Esmeralda. But had they been alive then, or were they already dead?

She went into the living room. The reproduction of Elvis was still hanging in its usual place. She lifted it away from the wall. If she had removed the wire, then she had replaced it so that no one would ever know, including herself.

She switched on the television and sat watching *I Love Lucy* reruns until it began to grow light outside.

Shortly after 8:00 A.M., Ralph called.

"Bonnie? Joyce Bach told me about Duke. You told me he left you. . . . I didn't realize that he was actually, like, *missing*."

"I don't know where he's gone, Ralph. I simply don't. And Ray, too. I had a nightmare last night that I murdered them."

"You sound terrible, if you don't mind my saying so."

"I feel terrible, Ralph. I feel terrible."

"Look—I think I've been very unfair. I've been blaming all of my problems on you. Phil Cafagna's a lecherous bastard, and in any case, businesswise, it was pretty stupid of me to put so many of my eggs into one basket."

"What does this mean, you've changed your mind?"

"It means, I feel like I've let you down. Like, used

you and then thrown you over. But it isn't like that, Bonnie. I swear it. When I said I loved you, I meant it."

"Well, maybe it was all for the best."

"Listen, Bonnie, why don't you meet me? We can talk."

"I'm not exactly one hundred percent today, Ralph."

"You're always one hundred percent to me, Bonnie. Please. At least give me the chance to explain myself."

Bonnie looked at the chrysalis inside the screw-top jar, almost ready to transform itself into a butterfly.

"Okay, then. Why don't you come around here?"

"You mean come to your home?"

"Why not? It's private, and the coffee's good."

"All right. All right, then. I'll see you at—what—twelve-fifteen?"

"I'll be here."

Bonnie put down the phone. She picked up the glass jar with the chrysalis and said, "What are you? What are you looking for? *Souls?* Why do we have to sacrifice the people we love the most? What do you get out of it?"

But in a strange way, she knew the answer to that. God had asked Abraham to kill his only son as a test of his belief. Maybe Itzpapalotl was doing the same.

RALPH POURS HIS HEART OUT

Before Ralph arrived, she went into the bedroom, drawing down the blinds and closing the shutters, so that it was almost completely dark. She turned the bed down and smoothed the bottom sheet, and then she placed the glass jar between the pillows and unscrewed the lid.

"You need someplace out of the light—I know that."

She closed the bedroom door and went back into the kitchen. She put on a pot of coffee to perk, and she arranged some shortbread and coconut cookies on a plate. Duke had always hated coconut.

She refreshed her makeup in front of the mirror and blew a kiss at Elvis. Almost at the same time, Ralph's glossy blue car arrived outside, and Ralph stepped out.

*　　*　　*

She dragged Duke off the sun lounger and into the house, his bare heels bumping on the carpet. Then she went back for Ray. She laid them side by side on the kitchen floor and closed and locked the sliding windows. Ray had a swollen, placid expression on his face, but Duke's eyes were wide open and he looked furious.

She went into the living room and unrolled the green vinyl sheeting over the carpet. It made a loud crackling noise as she crawled over it, making sure that it was well pinned down, underneath the chair legs.

She could have chosen to sacrifice Duke and Ray in the kitchen—nice white wipe-clean surface. But even though glazed pottery tiles are impervious, the grouting between them isn't, and even the minutest bloodstain could be found and tested for blood group and DNA.

Now she dragged their bodies into the living room and laid them next to each other and wrestled them out of their clothes. She was good at undressing inert and unhelpful bodies; she had done it almost every night with Duke. Once they were both lying naked on the floor, she went back to the kitchen to choose a carving knife, a black-handled Sabatier with a ten-inch blade.

"Bonnie?" asked Ralph. "Are you okay? I've said hello to you three times now, and you haven't answered once."

She blinked at him. She was standing by the open

door with a fixed smile on her face, not quite knowing how she had got there. "Ralph, hi."

"I feel really awkward about this."

"Awkward? Why should you feel awkward?"

"As always, I overreacted."

"It's a difficult situation, Ralph. You and me both
being married and all."

"Any news of Duke and Ray?"

"Nothing. Come on in. I've got beer, 7-Up, milk if
you want it."

Ralph came into the living room, glancing quickly
around with a mixture of curiosity and embar-
rassment. "Nice picture," he said, nodding toward
Elvis.

"It's great, isn't it? A friend of Duke's painted it."

He sat down on the edge of the couch. He was
wearing a putty-colored suit and a pink shirt and he
was perspiring.

"Want me to take your coat?" she asked him.

"No, thanks. I'm okay."

"You look really uncomfortable. Let me take
your coat."

"I'm fine, Bonnie, honestly. I can't stay long. But I
did want to square things between us."

"What's to square? I know you know that I didn't
make a pass at Phil Cafagna."

"You do?"

"You didn't end our relationship because of Phil
Cafagna. He canceled the order, for sure. But that
was just temper. He needs Glamorex products just
as much as Glamorex needs him. Where else is he
going to find a lip gloss that wholesales for a dollar-

twelve and retails for fifteen-ninety-nine? He'll be back, if he hasn't come back already."

Ralph said nothing, but took out a clean white handkerchief and dabbed his forehead.

"You lost your nerve, Ralph, that's all. I know that. It's a big step, leaving your partner and setting up with somebody else, especially when you're nearly forty and you're probably going to lose your house and your fancy new automobile and half of your business, too. I understand, Ralph. I thought it was going to change my life forever, as a matter of fact, but then, I have the same kind of responsibilities as you, don't I? Well, *had* . . . if Duke and Ray never come back."

"Where do you think they are, Bonnie?"

"I don't know, Ralph. I honestly don't."

"It seems kind of strange, doesn't it, that you can't even remember them leaving?"

"How do you know that?"

"What?"

"How do you know that I can't remember them leaving?"

"You told me. You told me yourself."

"I don't remember telling you that."

"Does it matter? What matters is, what happened to them?"

"I don't know, Ralph. I surely don't. Anyway, what are we talking about them for? I thought you came here to talk about *us*."

Ralph said, "I love you, Bonnie. You know that. But I've got too much to lose, and I'm too much of a coward to start all over."

"A coward, huh? I never would have had you down as a coward."

"I don't have the strength to change my life the way that you did."

"What does that mean? I didn't change my life."

"You—you know. You sorted out the Duke situation."

"I sorted out the Duke situation? I didn't do anything. The Duke situation sorted itself out by walking out the front door."

"But you didn't actually see him do that, did you?"

Bonnie turned around on the couch and frowned at him. "What kind of a conversation is this, Ralph?"

"I'm proud of you for dealing with it, that's all."

"I didn't do anything. I went to sleep in the evening, and when I woke up in the morning he was gone."

"Bonnie—"

She pressed an orange-polished fingertip to his lips. "You don't have to say anything, Ralph. You don't have to say anything at all, except 'I love you.' You're right—my life is changed now. I'm single. I'm alone. I don't have anybody. I've been thinking about this . . . wondering what I'd say if you called me. And I knew you'd call me. But I don't have what it takes to break up a marriage, do I? That's what you wanted to say. Well, I don't mind that. I can live with that, so long as we go on seeing each other. You can stay married to your empty suitcase, and you can keep your house and your car and all of your investments. I'll stay here alone. So long as we can meet and make love whenever you have the time, and so long as I know that it's me you really want, and not Vanessa, then I can live with that situation, and be happy with it."

Ralph stared at her. "Are you serious?"

"Do I sound like I'm joking?"

"I don't know what to say, Bonnie. I honestly don't."

She kissed him on the lips. "Why don't you say nothing at all? Why don't you come to bed with me, and show me that everything's going to work out fine?"

Ralph was sweating so much that he had to wipe his forehead with his sleeve. "Bonnie . . . your husband's missing. . . . He could be dead."

"What do you care? What do I care? He was lazy and violent and bigoted and drunk, and our son was growing up the same way."

"That wasn't any reason to kill him, though, was it?"

Bonnie sat up straight. "What's the matter with you, Ralph?"

"I just said that wasn't any reason to kill him."

Bonnie offered her hand. "Come into the bedroom, Ralph. Let's forget about Duke. Let's start thinking about us."

"I—uh—I don't have the time."

"You don't have the *time*? Of course you have the time."

She took hold of both his hands and pulled him up off the couch. Then she led him across the living room to the bedroom door.

"Bonnie—"

"I want to show you something, Ralph. I want to

show you something really amazing. Are you ready for this?"

"Listen, Bonnie, I have a critical lunch appointment. I only came over to—"

Bonnie squeezed his hand tightly, so that he couldn't break free. She stood on tiptoe and kissed him, and smiled at him. "Come and see what's in here."

She turned the knob and opened the door. Inside the bedroom it was almost totally dark. Bonnie kept on smiling, but Ralph hesitated and tried to tug his hand away.

"What's that noise?" he asked her.

Bonnie listened. Yes, she could hear it, too. A papery rustling noise, then a very soft, high-pitched chittering sound. Then a scraping, like knife blades being drawn across each other.

"Come and take a look," Bonnie insisted.

"I don't think so. What is it? There's something in there, isn't there? What is it?"

"Come see for yourself."

There was another scraping sound, and then a loud, hurried flutter, like a large moth beating desperately against a paper lampshade. That was when Ralph lost it.

"Get me out of here!" he screamed. "For Christ's sake, you guys, get me out of here!"

Bonnie slammed the bedroom door shut. "Who are you talking to?" she demanded. "Who are you talking to, Ralph? What guys?"

Ralph tried to struggle away from her, but Bonnie yanked his coat off his shoulders, and there they were: a wire and a microphone.

"You're wired," she said, in utter disgust. "You said you loved me and you're *wired!*"

A second later, the front door burst open and Dan Munoz came in, followed by Detective Mesic and four uniformed police officers. Ralph pulled away from Bonnie and retreated to the other side of the room, looking miserable and bruised. Dan came up to Bonnie and gave her a regretful smile.

"You want to tell me what this is all about?" Bonnie asked him, still trembling with anger. "That man was supposed to be my lover."

"I know," said Dan, gently. "That was why he was the best choice."

"The best choice for what? To get me to incriminate myself for a crime that hasn't even been committed yet?"

"Oh, it's been committed all right. That's why we're here. I have to admit that I was hoping for a taped confession, but there's plenty of circumstantial."

"Like what? A knife that's cleaner than you think it ought to be? Do you want to indict me for having a spotless toilet as well?"

"We've found the bodies," said Dan.

Bonnie went utterly cold. "You've found them? Duke and Ray? Both of them?"

Dan took hold of her elbow. "You've got a strong stomach. Come and take a look. Mesic—check the bedroom."

"Where are they? How did they die?"

"Come on, we'll take you there. You can see for yourself."

Detective Mesic opened the bedroom door. "Pretty dark in here. Hold on, I'll open the shutters."

He opened the shutters and let up the blinds, and the bedroom was flooded with sunlight. Mesic opened the closets and banged them shut again and tugged out two or three dressing-table drawers. "Nothing here, sir."

Ralph gave Bonnie the strangest look, but he didn't say anything.

Dan ushered her toward the door.

DUKE AND RAY SHOW UP

On the southeastern side of the Riverside waste facility, in the middle of a stinking mountain range of domestic garbage, they came across four patrol cars, two medical examiner's station wagons and an ambulance, all parked neatly in line, as if they were attending a sporting event. Dan pulled up alongside them.

"You found them *here*?" asked Bonnie.

"We found them here because we were looking for them here. We also had a pretty good idea of exactly when they were dumped."

He opened the car door for her, and together they walked across flattened cereal packets, split-open diapers, compressed cans of Green Giant sweet corn. The midday smog was made even worse by the ran-

cid smoke that leaked out of burning piles of rubbish.
Detective Mesic started to cough.

There was no real need for words. Dan took Bonnie's elbow and steered her toward the front of the
little crowd of police officers and medical examiners
and photographers, and there they were. Duke and
Ray, side by side, like gunned-down bank robbers
from the Old West propped up in their coffins.

They weren't lying in coffins, however. They were
lying in ripped-open, heavily bloodstained mattresses. The mattresses from George Keighley's house,
on which David Hinsey and Maria Carranza had
died. They were both naked, both immensely
bloated, and both teeming with maggots. Their chests
had been cut wide open, and Duke had been emascu-
lated. Between his legs he wore a codpiece of glittering blowflies.

Bonnie stood and stared at them for a long time.
Dan folded his arms and waited for her, patiently.

"You told me you disposed of the mattresses *before*
you drove home," Dan reminded her. "But since you
were so uncertain of your schedule, I had it checked
through. I found out that you didn't actually come here
to deposit these mattresses until four forty-seven P.M.,
not long before the facility was due to close for the day.

"You made a phone call at home to Esmeralda at
three oh two P.M. I suspect that Duke and Ray were
already dead by then. All you had to do was cut the
mattresses open, roll their bodies inside, stitch them
up roughly, and drive them down here to the dump.
They could have been bulldozed over and buried
here forever."

Bonnie looked at Duke's swollen, distorted face, and at Ray's, but they didn't even look like her husband and her son anymore. "It was Itzpapalotl," she said, very quietly. "I asked her for help. I asked her for a way out. So she came, and she set me free, free like she is, like a butterfly."

ANSWERING MACHINE MESSAGE

"Bonnie . . . this is Howard Jacobson. You remember, you brought me that caterpillar not long ago. *Parnassius mnemonsyne*, the Clouded Apollo. You may be interested to know that the larvae were brought over in several large consignments of Mexican kale. Because of the unusual weather conditions, especially El Niño, they hatched out and prospered, and we've had reports of them as far afield as Santa Barbara and Bakersfield. They don't really have any relevance to our specialty, I'm afraid . . . determining the time of death . . . but you can't win them all, can you? Don't be a stranger, love, Howard."

NIGHT FALLS

That night, Bonnie was awakened by a rustling sound. She turned over, grunting; but then she heard it again. She opened her eyes and sat up.

Standing in the darkest corner of her cell was a figure with an expressionless white face and wings with glittering edges. The figure made the softest of whirring noises, and its feet scratched on the concrete floor, as if it had claws.

"Itzpapalotl," Bonnie whispered.

The figure came nearer and leaned over her, spreading its wings wider. She could see its eyes now, and a tongue that shone like a black-bladed knife.

"Take me with you," said Bonnie. "Please, Itzpapalotl. Take me with you."

GET OUT OF JAIL FREE

They had searched her, of course—but they had reckoned without her intimate knowledge of the ingenious ways in which people can end their own lives. When they opened the cell door at 6:03 A.M. the next morning, they found her lying on her back, staring at the ceiling in the same way that she had stared at the ceiling on the day Duke disappeared, except that there was an ever-widening pool of blood spreading across the floor of her cell, and she was dead.

She had pulled one of the buttons off her mattress and burrowed into the kapok filling with her fingernails, tugging out one of the springs. Then she had used the sharp end of the spring to tear open the veins in both her wrists.

At 11:17 A.M., Lieutenant Dan Munoz came into her cell to look at her. He stood by the door for a long time, wondering what it was that had brought her to this.

He didn't notice two butterflies with almost colorless wings, which had been perched on the steel mesh that covered the windows. After he had been standing there for a while, they fluttered out the door and along the corridor, then out through the bars to the open air, and the morning sunshine, and freedom.